Then
There Grew Up
a Generation . . .

Books by Thyra Ferré Bjorn

PAPA'S WIFE

PAPA'S DAUGHTER

MAMA'S WAY

A Trilogy, containing

PAPA'S WIFE, PAPA'S
DAUGHTER *and* MAMA'S WAY

DEAR PAPA

ONCE UPON A
CHRISTMAS TIME

THIS IS MY LIFE

THE HOME HAS A HEART

THEN THERE GREW UP
A GENERATION . . .

Then
There Grew Up
a Generation...

❧ ❧ ❧

THYRA FERRÉ BJORN

❧

HOLT, RINEHART AND WINSTON

NEW YORK   CHICAGO   SAN FRANCISCO

Published simultaneously in Canada by
Holt, Rinehart and Winston of Canada, Limited

Library of Congress Catalog Card Number: 74-117285

Published, September, 1970
Second Printing, October, 1970

Designer: Ernst Reichl

SBN: 03-085050-9
Printed in the United States of America

To Folke and Elaine
with love

Then

There Grew Up

a Generation . . .

❧ 1

THE REVEREND Mark Cartling was halfway down the hill when he stopped and looked back at the church. How majestic and proud it stood—how white, with its tall spire gracing the sky. A warmth flooded Mark as he remembered its history, dating back into the eighteenth century, though it had been rebuilt and modernized many times.

He leaned against the stone wall which followed the walk to the level part of the street. His heart was light today, as though a joyous melody were singing within him. He smiled to himself as he thought of yesterday's sermon still lying in its folder on the shelf under the pulpit in the sanctuary. It was the most powerful sermon he had ever written. Bold and black, its topic stood out against the white paper—"And Then There Grew up a Generation Who Knew Not God." It had taken him hours to finish it and he had worked long into the night as he had scanned the Old Testament in search of material. It was there he had found his text. Compelled by a harsh desire to preach the truth, he had written words against his will. He had made a firm decision that it was his obligation to reveal to his congregation his conviction that the church of God had fallen. It was no longer a power in the community, nor was it a pathfinder for the young. He had to warn his people—even scare them if necessary—to make them see that The Church, his church, their church, had become a power-hungry, self-centered organization which had lost its usefulness. Mark had not minced words; his sermon spoke in hard, strong phrases, meant to penetrate deep into the minds and souls of those in the pews.

But he had never preached that sermon. The words he had committed to paper remained unspoken. That Sunday morning had started out in a strange gloom, he had felt that Heaven was made of brass and that there was no way to communicate with the Almighty. Then suddenly it had changed. In the darkness there had come light. It was as though unseen hands had lifted from his shoulders the burden of two years, and he had found a glorious answer to all his doubts. It was a miracle! The greatest miracle he had ever experienced in his entire ministry! Even now as he thought back to what had happened only yesterday, it was hard to believe.

Mark began to walk again slowly, keeping a mental image of the church on the hilltop. Bathed in sunshine, it seemed like a heavenly benediction, a great amen.

2

Perhaps now, he was thinking, it would become a holy hill, as those devout men and women who had raised the first small church had called it. It was with hard labor, sweat, sacrifice, and prayer that they had completed their task. But that was long ago and that small, humble house of prayer had become a plush church, rich in gold and worldly possessions, well-known in the East. And he, Mark Cartling, was the head minister here in this Community Church at Robendale-by-the-Sea with a membership of well over two thousand and new people joining as families moved into the area. It was "the church" to belong to and its ministers were popular, charming, respected, and loved by young and old alike. At least that was the way it was supposed to be, and even if the love for one of the pastoral family began to cool, people outside would never know.

It had been three years since the Cartlings moved here. They had come from a small mill town in New Hampshire; from a small, plain church whose congregation increased measurably in summer when vacationers swarmed the mountainside. Mark would always believe that some of the summer people had given his name to the pulpit committee at Robendale-by-the-Sea. The first call had been simply to preach a sermon on a Sunday morning. Mark had been much impressed by the size and beauty of the church and the fine, receptive congregation. But as weeks passed with no further word, he had given up all thoughts of ever hearing from them again. When the call finally came, it had taken him by surprise. He could not believe that they had really chosen him to be their new pastor, even over some candidates with higher degrees and more experience. But it was Mark Cartling they wanted.

Had it been presumptuous of him to believe that they had selected him because of his speaking ability, his rare gift of imagery, his talent for capturing and holding his listeners' attention whatever the reason, he had been delighted, humble, and grateful and had promised himself that he would do everything in his power to live up to their expectations. The first year in Robendale had been a fruitful, happy one; it had taken him and his family that long to find their place in the community and to learn the names and faces of their upper middle-class congregation, many of them quite wealthy. Mark found them congenial and interesting. It had seemed that he had the ideal parish; then without warning his world had begun to crumble. Instead of peace, there was strife; instead of cooperation and understanding, the members began to split into two groups—for him and against him. It had hurt him to see it coming and at times he had felt like a drowning man crying out for help.

Now as Mark took long strides toward the park leading down to the sea, dark memories of the hurt and humiliation he had suffered took form. He would have to try to erase them, putting them against the account of the church in the world today.

Mark was a handsome man, tall and strong, with dark hair and brown eyes that were gentle and kind most of

4

the time, but which became black and forbidding when his soul was in an uproar. They were black now as he thought about the changing church and its effect on the ministry. It was the minister who bore the brunt of it, he thought. It was he who became the sacrificial offering for a selfish generation. Was it any wonder that so many left their churches to seek professions offering peace of mind and security. But in Mark Cartling's eyes it was a false security. He had no sympathy for men who retreated when they should have been pressing forward. It was the persistent who would finally conquer this sickness that had taken over the world, and those who were willing to fight their way through a fog of blindness would win out. The servants of the Most High must trust their God in spite of the changing world, and they must know that whatever else changes, God is the same yesterday, today, and tomorrow.

A sense of tranquillity filled Mark's soul when he saw the blue ocean and heard the tiny waves lapping against the shore. God's mind was deeper than the ocean; it was higher than the heavens and wider than the world, and those who trusted their God would see a light in the darkness just as he had in this very church. Now Mark was ready for his real work in the world, and he knew he would not be alone. Most of those who had dedicated their lives to service yesterday would join him in offering brotherhood to mankind, helping to lift those who had stumbled. And that would be his story. After all, wasn't all earth life a story? Wasn't it written in laughter and tears, sunshine and shadows? Each new generation wrote its own story, trying to make it a little brighter than the one before, catching for themselves the brilliance of the rainbow, holding onto its glow until the next generation began to wrestle it away from them. To Mark, today's generation seemed to push and shove more vigorously than any previous one, storming any weak defense to gain its own way in a topsy-turvy world.

And the Church was caught in the midst of the chaos, thrown back and forth like a storm-tossed ship, with each minister seeking to find his own way to bring his church through in one piece. Each day a new story was written, but not one had escaped the impact of humiliation and confusion that made them wonder: Where are we going from here? Will the Church be able to stand in the world of tomorrow? But Mark knew that in spite of all, an army of Christians would carry out that commission given to the first church— to go out into the world to light a light, to make people disciples, to usher in a Kingdom which would see an end to war, sin, and soul-sickness . . . a Kingdom bringing stability, freedom, and peace.

An important chapter of the Cartling family's story began on a beautiful June day when they moved to Robendale-by-the-Sea, and looking back now they knew that the preceding years had been just a preparation. They were a happy family of five. Susan, the oldest child, was sixteen, the image of her blonde, blue-eyed, Scandinavian mother. David, next in line, was fifteen; and Eric, the youngest, had just celebrated his tenth birthday. Elsa Cartling had a mystic charm all her own. A warm, friendly manner, enhanced by beauty, made her a real bonus to her husband and his work. She was a good mother, adored by her children, and a fine wife, perfectly suited to her role as a minister's wife.

That June day had been an exciting one for the Cartlings as they drove up the hill toward the church, unmistakably visible from all directions. The streets were shaded by ancient elm trees, so typical of an old New England town. When they reached the top of the hill, Mark parked the car and the family sat silently for a moment looking at the beautiful old white church.

"Well, what do you think?" asked Mark, looking lovingly at his somewhat stunned family.

"Oh, Mark," answered Elsa, "I never dreamed that it would be so beautiful. What an elegant church!"

Mark smiled. "I told you it was one of the most beautiful churches in New England. It's not just the building, but the lawns and shrubbery. And the view . . . you could never tire of that—the sea so close—and even that funny stone wall following the walk down the hill. What a place this is! I'll be the envy of many ministers."

"I'm glad now," said Elsa, "that I didn't come down here to see it before. It's wonderful to be so pleasantly surprised."

"Is this really your church, Daddy?" asked Susan.

"Yes, my dear. Just look at that sign—'The Reverend Mark Cartling, Senior Pastor.'"

"It's really tops, Dad," said David.

"A neat church all right," approved Eric. "May we go inside?"

"Let's save that until later. I know your mother is anxious to see the parsonage."

It was only a few minutes' drive from the church to the parsonage, and if the family had been delighted with the church, they were overwhelmed by their new home—a large colonial white-frame house, magnificently nestled among evergreens. Rambling roses cascaded over a rustic wooden fence that enclosed a spacious green lawn. Everything breathed of gracious living, as the sun sparkled on window panes framed by snow-white ruffled curtains.

"Oh, Mark," said Elsa, "what a place to move your family into! I feel as though I'm dreaming this whole thing."

Mark laughed. "I've had a hard time keeping the details a surprise for you, but this is it—our new town, our church, and our very own parsonage. But I suppose I'll always wonder why I happened to be chosen."

"It was no surprise to me, Mark. Even if our last church was small, your sermons are the best in the land."

"And couldn't my wife be just a little bit prejudiced? After all, she's listened to me for almost eighteen years. But I hope you're right, Elsa. I hope people will think I'm a good speaker. But come, let's go inside."

Mark unlocked the front door and they stepped into a

8

large flag-stone foyer separating the large living room and dining room.

"Is this furniture to be ours, too?" asked Elsa.

Mark nodded.

"It's beautiful, Mark, especially that big round dining-room table. And just look at that bouquet of flowers! Someone has been very thoughtful. Is that a note in it?"

Mark took the note from the flowers and opened it.

"We're invited out for dinner," he announced. "My lady will not have to cook on this first day. All of us are to be the guests of my associate pastor, Bill Lowell, and his wife, who are, by the way, a couple of newlyweds."

"This is spoiling me, Mark! I'm apt to become lazy and demanding in such luxury and ease."

Mark looked at Elsa tenderly. "I doubt that. There'll be very little time for laziness with all the duties that will fall on you in this town, and I think it will take a little more than a beautiful parsonage to throw you off balance, my dear."

Soon the children reappeared from their exploration of their new home.

"Oh, Daddy," cried Susan, wrapping her arms around Mark's neck. "I'm so happy I think I'm going to cry. I've seen my room and it's just perfect with an old-fashioned canopy bed and everything. Where did all that beautiful furniture come from?"

"That's quite a story," said Mark. "A wealthy old lady, whose ancestors were members of this church's first congregation and who, I understand, gave most of the money to build this parsonage, willed the furniture to the church when she died six months ago. We're the first family to use it."

David flopped down into a high-backed leather chair. "Gosh," he said, "I just wish all the kids in New Hampshire could see this pad. I know I'll miss the mountains, but maybe the ocean will make up for it."

"As soon as we're settled, you can have your whole gang down here," said Elsa. "How about a cook out on the beach?"

"That would be great, Mom!"

Eric was quiet, his forehead furrowed in a deep frown.

"What's the matter, Skipper?" asked Mark. "Don't you like it here?"

"It's okay, Dad, but it's all so fancy. You know how much I want a dog, but how can I have a dog in this house?"

Elsa patted his blond head.

"Don't worry about it, son! If you have a dog in this house, you can be sure it will be no ordinary mut. But what will stop us from getting a pedigree dog?"

Eric beamed from ear to ear; no words could have pleased him more.

Suddenly Elsa remembered something. "Mark, have you forgotten the moving van? It should be arriving here any time now. What are we going to do with all that old furniture?"

"We'll have to store it," answered Mark. "Remember, all this is just lend-lease while we're living here. When we move on to the next place, we'll probably have to

10

have our own furniture again. They assured me there was adequate space to store everything here."

"There's a big storage room in the basement," said David. "I'm sure we could put our stuff down there."

Down to the basement they all went to investigate. And it seemed that David was right. There was plenty of room for all of their things.

Dinner that night with the Lowells was delightful. They were a lot of fun, and Mark and Elsa felt that already a warm friendship had started between them even though the associate pastor and his wife, Carol, were so much younger than the Cartlings.

It had been such a good beginning. Mark and Elsa had agreed on that after the children were in bed and they had retired to their spacious room with its heavy satin rose drapes that closed out the shadows of night. A stillness fell over the room as Elsa seemed to be resting comfortably in the large double bed. It had taken her only a moment to fall asleep.

She will be happy here, thought Mark to himself. For a while she'll think she's in a fairyland, but she'll have lots of fun playing her part. He wondered if she had given New Hampshire a thought. Had she too felt a little pang of homesickness for the old parsonage they had left only this morning? It had been their home for six years. It was true that the house had been cold and drafty in winter and that it had needed a lot of repairs, but they had been happy there. Their people had been the salt of the earth—simple, hard-working, good people. How kind they had always been. Mark was sure he had left the church in better shape than it had been when he arrived. The membership had increased; the people were spiritually stronger. In that way he felt he had fulfilled his duty. But had it been right to leave them? That question bothered him tonight, as he pictured the little gray church standing there beside the cemetery without a shepherd for its flock.

A strange loneliness gripped him. Why was it always right for a pastor to leave a poor little church for a rich large one? Those people meant so well and struggled so hard to better their community. And what a fine farewell reception they had given the Cartling family. A large purse, far more than they could afford, had been given to him. Elsa had been given a beautiful pin, and each of the children had received a gift. In his mind, Mark could hear familiar voices and see the dear faces. The words of the Chairman of the Board of Deacons had touched him deeply, and some of them he would never forget.

"We have known for a long time," Mr. Swan had said in his halting speech, "that our little church could not keep a pastor like Mark Cartling for any length of time. But we thank you for the years you have spent with us and we wish you God's blessing as you go on to wider fields and richer grounds. . . ."

Deacon Swan's words were still on Mark's mind as he drifted off to sleep. Over and over again they repeated themselves: wider fields . . . richer grounds . . . and Mark Cartling, too, had fallen into a deep sleep.

12

❧ 2

THAT FIRST YEAR for the Cartlings at Robendale-by-the-Sea seemed to pass almost too quickly. Elsa was amazed to see how easily the children had adjusted to their new surroundings; it was as though New Hampshire had never been. All three of them seemed to have found their niche. Little Eric seemed to have forgotten about having a dog once he had found a friend just his own age, the son of the rabbi. The Danewiches lived just three houses away from the Cartlings and Eric and Bernie were inseparable. David had developed a strong interest in experimenting. He had been given a small storeroom in the basement to use as a laboratory, and he worked afternoons for the town pharmacy, doing odd jobs to earn enough money to buy his miracle-working ingredients. David seemed to enjoy being alone, and although he had a few friends, he seemed content with or without them. At times Elsa worried about David, but Mark assured her that he was just

13

going through teen-age growing pains which would disappear as he grew older. David seemed happy in his own world of self-imposed solitude.

Susan was, perhaps, the happiest of the three. She had found a steady boyfriend, Gary O'Brien, who was her whole world. They had met the first week of school that previous September when Gary was a senior and Susan a junior.

Both Elsa and Mark had tried in vain to discourage this involvement. Gary was a fine boy—tall, handsome, muscular, and an honor student—but he belonged to the Church of the Sacred Heart, and the Cartlings would much rather have had Susan choose a boy of her own faith. As things stood now, Susan occasionally attended Mass with Gary on Sunday morning; at other times he accompanied her to the Community Church.

"You see, Mom," Susan had explained to Elsa, "if Gary and I should ever marry, we don't want any division. We've already discussed that. One of us would accept the other's faith. That is why we must learn about each other's church."

Elsa had to agree that it sounded fair, but she couldn't help feeling that Susan was much too young even to think about marriage. Young people were so unpredictable and so idealistic and fell in and out of love so many times that Elsa doubted that Susan would ever marry Gary.

But the big event at present was the Senior Prom. Susan was, of course, going with Gary and the shopping expedition for that special dress had been a delightful adventure. Susan had finally settled on a sky-blue creation that would add to the sparkle of her eyes. Susan's life was full and eventful and had never been happier.

June fifth, the night of the Senior Prom, was especially exciting to the graduating class, even if to the rest of the world it was just another summer night of balmy breezes softly swaying the treetops. Tonight a big yellow moon hung in the sky, looking with apparent approval on the earth below. It was the kind of moon Elsa wanted to ignore as she thought of her daughter strolling somewhere with a certain young man. The young people would be everywhere tonight—in parked cars and on secluded park benches—and that moon would only add to the air of romance. In the early morning hours, most of them would gather for a snack at the all-night restaurant on Pearl Street, the Do-Drop-In, appropriately decorated for the occasion with colored balloons and flowers.

But Elsa could not sleep. She watched the hands on her clock as she lay very still beside Mark whose even breathing indicated deep slumber. For hours now she had remained motionless for fear of arousing Mark. Then he stirred in his sleep, and she was almost sure he was awakening. He might speak to her any second now, and she knew very well just what he would say. At this very moment she felt that she needed the wisdom of Solomon to speak the right words. Nothing in the world must mar Susan's happiness tonight, not even Mark.

Perhaps she was only a foolish mother who, for the

15

first time, had broken the bond that she and Mark had always had as parents. They had an understanding that they would always discuss anything concerning their children. Their decisions were to be made together, and Elsa knew she had not said even one word to Mark about tonight. Was that what it was like to be the mother of a teen-age girl? Was she more mother than wife? And if she couldn't be both, which was more important? It had all happened because she had been so sure that Mark would have put his foot down. Elsa just didn't want to see laws made that she knew Susan would break.

Oh, she thought with a little pang of remorse, if only Mark could have seen the stars in Susan's eyes when she and Gary came down to the basement laundry room that afternoon last week.

Gary had been loaded down with books which he plunked nonchalantly on the dryer before he himself flopped down on the lowest step.

"Mrs. Cartling," he had begun, taking Susan's hand in his, "Susan and I have something very important to ask you."

Elsa had stopped pressing her dress. For a moment her heart had stood still. They were too young, she had thought, altogether too young even to think of marriage.

"It's about the prom next week. May we have your permission to stay out all night?"

"All night, Gary?" she had questioned, secretly relieved that that was all they wanted.

"Yes, Mrs. Cartling. All the kids are planning to do it.

Most of them aren't even going to ask their parents' permission, for fear they might say no. But Susan and I wanted to check it out."

Reason told her not to promise anything too quickly; she knew she should talk this over with Susan's father first and that he probably would say no. But before she had let herself think rationally, her lips had already agreed.

"Well, I suppose if everyone is going to stay up all night I can't deny you the same privilege. And I *am* glad you asked. I appreciate that."

In a flash Susan's arms had been around her, nearly knocking over the ironing board.

"Oh, Mom, you're a peach! I just love you more than anyone else in the whole world! Thank you, Mom. With you as a mother, it's not so hard to be a preacher's kid."

"You'll never be sorry that you trusted us," beamed Gary, putting his arm around Elsa too.

After they had gone, Elsa had felt good all over. They were so sweet and honest! What else could she have done but grant their request? It had all seemed so right then; not until tonight had she begun to wonder about the wisdom of her decision. The *whole* night was a long, long time.

The grandfather's clock in the hall struck five times.

Suddenly Mark sat up in bed. "Elsa, was that five o'clock?" he asked. "Have you heard Susan come in?"

"No, I don't think she's in yet. This is the Senior Prom, you know. The kids are usually out very late on prom nights."

17

"And you're not worried about her? I'm sure other mothers are pacing the floor, and here you are, cool as a cucumber. I just don't understand it, Elsa."

Elsa did not answer Mark immediately; but when her words came, they were calm and gentle. Mark couldn't know how violently her heart was pounding.

"Mark, I've been thinking all night; I just couldn't sleep. Our Susan is almost grown up now, and she's been going with Gary for a year. He's a fine boy. Mark, we live in modern times; we're dealing with the children of tomorrow's world. We must be careful not to drive them away from us."

"And what does that mean? That we should let them do as they please? Without any direction or discipline?"

"No, dear, but we have to make exceptions, like to-night when all the kids are going to stay out all night. Susan wanted to be out too, and I told her that if all the others were doing it, she needn't be the only one who had to come home and go to bed."

"*You* told her, Elsa, without even talking to me about it? That isn't like you. Haven't we always decided things about the children together?"

Elsa knew that Mark was deeply hurt.

"Perhaps I was wrong, Mark, but I was afraid you wouldn't see it my way. So for the first time, I made up my mind alone. I wanted Susan to have fun tonight and not to be restricted because she was the minister's daughter. Perhaps I am just a foolish mother. You know, it was strange. For just that moment when I said yes to Susan, I was more mother than wife. There must be

18

times in everyone's household when something like that happens. Please don't be angry with me, Mark."

She could feel Mark's arm reaching out for her, and soon she was enclosed in his embrace. Everything would be all right now; she had won. Mark would not be cross with Susan, no matter how late she came in.

Elsa relaxed a little, thinking that her husband had gone back to sleep when he spoke again. His voice was tender, but firm. She knew that what he was saying came from deep conviction and that he wanted her to understand that.

"Elsa, you might think you've won tonight because I haven't stormed around accusing you of overriding my judgment, but that's not so, my dear. Something in our relationship with Susan has been broken. We've lost our hold on her decisions, and from now on, she won't even ask. She'll choose her own path. It's true that she's seventeen and not interested in the way things were in our youth. She wants the freedom to live in her own time. But don't you see, dear, what mothers will say who have denied their daughters the privilege of a whole night's freedom only to find that the minister's daughter has that very freedom. What shall I tell them, Elsa?"

"Just tell them you had nothing to do with it, Mark. Tell them the truth, that your wife never consulted you, but gave Susan the permission on her own."

"I might have to do that, Elsa. I might have to. My position is not an easy one."

Elsa thought about Mark's words long after he had

gone back to sleep, and she wasn't happy. Had she done the wrong thing? What did she want for Susan? Was it popularity, fun, and an easy life? Or was it strength of character, wisdom in making decisions, and convictions strong enough to make her give up something for the good of others? What did she really, really want for Susan?

Hearing a car door slam, Elsa left her bed and tiptoed to the hall window, which was open. She heard Susan's voice saying, "Gary, the night has been perfect. I've never been happier."

"And you, Susan, are the greatest. I'll love you always. This night was ours, Susan—just ours."

There was quiet for a long, long moment. Then Susan let herself in the front door. She did not see her mother as she ran up the stairs and into her room, closing the door noiselessly behind her.

A happy girl bubbling over with life, thought Elsa as she walked back into her own room. Yes, she's the happiest girl in the world tonight—just seventeen with her whole life ahead of her, thinking herself madly in love with a handsome boy.

Sleep would not come to Elsa immediately. Her conscience bothered her, and she still wondered whether or not she had done the right thing. She couldn't forget Mark's last words. Would her own foolishness mold her daughter into a self-indulgent person, needing neither the help nor the advice of her parents? Perhaps it would have been better if she had talked the matter over with Mark, letting him decide, even if he said no.

Susan had changed in the last few months. She was

no longer interested in the youth group at the church. She always found some excuse for not attending the meetings. She had never taken Gary to a Sunday-night activity. Elsa had always considered high-school love a fleeting thing, but now she wondered. She was glad that in another year Susan would be preparing for college. Perhaps there she would find another romance. Elsa wanted Susan to have a happy home of her own some-day, but she also wanted her to marry a man of her own faith.

But just now she need not worry about it. Susan was back in her own room. Elsa could visualize her asleep, her long dark lashes resting like half moons on her flushed cheeks. She could see Susan's blonde hair ruf-fled, as it always was in slumber, with a few stray curls stealing down her forehead. Warmth flooded Elsa's heart. Susan was beautiful and sweet; she must not worry about her. Today's young people had to have freedom; they demanded it, sometimes nicely as was Susan's way and Gary's; sometimes by taking it. The younger generation made it clear that they wanted no fences erected which they might have to break down. They were a strong-willed group, and if only they used that will in the right way, they could be the greatest generation ever to have lived.

In the midst of her thought, Elsa realized that Mark was awake, too.

"So she finally came in," he said.

"Yes, dear, she's safe in her own bed now. After all, Mark, a first formal only happens once in a lifetime."

He patted her arm.

"Try to catch a little sleep, Elsa." Mark's voice was tender. "Irma will be here early, and I'll leave a note asking her to take care of the children's breakfast so you can sleep."

"Thank you, Mark. That will be wonderful! And thank you for understanding."

Elsa closed her eyes. The house was very quiet. It was a good house and the whole family seemed so safe there. All had gone well and Mark had not been angry, thought Elsa as she drifted off.

~ 3

PASTOR CARTLING WAS, as a rule, an early riser, but this morning he was late. It was past nine by the time he had finished showering and dressing and was ready to leave for his study. Elsa was still fast asleep. For a moment Mark had the urge to awaken her just to see her warm parting smile that always seemed to make his day start right. But he restrained himself, remembering the troubled night she had spent because of Susan. Lovingly he looked down at her sleeping face, which still held the expression of an anxious, bewildered child.

Poor darling, Mark thought. She did have a rough time last night. It isn't easy to be a mother and a wife at the same time, especially when the rules work at cross purposes.

His hand touched her soft blonde hair lightly, pushing it back from her forehead. It was strange how just touching her filled him with warmth and peace. He had that jubilant assurance that she belonged to him and him alone.

23

Surely now, when the trouble concerning the prom was over, things in the parsonage would return to normal. It was lucky that this was Saturday and that Irma, the woman who did their weekly cleaning, had come early that morning. She had already completed some of her chores and was now serving breakfast to the two younger children. Mark could hear David and Eric chattering as he started down the wide stairway.

Their voices came from the kitchen clearly.

"I'm not kidding you, Irma!" Eric said. "David's going to be the first man on Mars! You tell her, Dave."

"Yeah, I am Irma, but don't let the secret out. At least not until I get my spaceship tested."

Irma's hearty laughter echoed through the house. "You mean it, Dave, don't you? But won't you have some competition from the nation's space program?"

"No, they're only going to the moon so far. And I'm working on my ship day and night, now that I have my laboratory in the basement. It was kind of dangerous having all those explosives up in my room."

"For goodness' sake, Dave, how can you get a whole spaceship anywhere inside of the house?"

"Oh, this is just a model. It's pretty small, but it's powerful. It could blow a hole right through the parsonage roof if I weren't so careful. You see, a person has to know about explosives—how to handle them and where to keep them so no one gets at them. Eric is the only one who knows. I let him in on my secret, and now there's you, Irma. But you wouldn't talk about it, would you?"

"Certainly not, Dave, if you promise me a trip when the big ship is ready—that is, if I live that long."

"You'll live that long all right. I'm coming along real well because I know just what to do now. It isn't the work or the time; it's what you know that counts."

"But where do you get the explosives?"

"Oh, I know where to buy them, and I work for Mr. Dilling after school to earn the money to pay for them. You know, I empty trash and put away boxes of stuff. Oh, by the way, Mr. Dilling knows about the spaceship, too. And his wife might . . . you never know what a man will tell his wife."

"That's for sure!" laughed Irma. "But I always thought you were going to be a preacher like your dad."

"Nah, not me. There's no future for preachers. They're fading out of the picture. People don't really need them any more. They're more or less of a luxury. But outer space, Irma—spaceships—that's the thing for us kids. That's what the future is all about. I feel sorry for Dad sometimes. Don't misunderstand me. He's a swell guy and he's doing a swell job here, but he has no future because soon there'll be no one to preach to. Everyone will have taken off somewhere to do their thing. It's going to be a groovy new world, Irma; you just wait and see."

Mark changed his mind about going through the kitchen to say good morning to the children. At first he had even thought he might have breakfast with them. But now he decided to have a bite to eat at the drugstore, pick up the morning paper, and get to the church study quickly. He closed the front door noiselessly behind him.

Once outside, Mark laughed to himself. And last

night he and Elsa had worried about Susan being out all night. What would she think now if she knew that David, her golden boy, was about to take off for Mars? Poor parents of these children of today!

There was a frown between Mark's eyebrows. For some reason he could not dismiss David's words. "I feel sorry for Dad," David had confided to Irma.

So there was no future in that preaching stuff? That was what his son was thinking in that bright brain of his. He had probably formulated these thoughts while he sat there in church Sunday mornings listening to his father's sermons. And Mark had always believed that his son was proud of him, that someday he would step into his father's shoes and wear his mantle. So people would not have time for religion, eh? They would have no need for preachers. It certainly was a strange, complicated world his son was living in. He might as well have confessed that parents, too, were unnecessary for the self-styled intelligent person growing up in the present. They were a luxury, perhaps, like preachers. What did Dave, deep down in his own ever-working brain, think of parents? Perhaps someday his father would be brave enough to ask him.

Mark had a cup of coffee at the town pharmacy where David worked after school. That business about the explosives was probably just a wild story to impress Irma. But just the same, you almost could have believed the kid, the way he had explained it.

Secrets, thought Mark, vital secrets going on in the parsonage, affecting members of his family, and the

26

pastor was not supposed to know a thing about them. Well, it was kid stuff and he had to regard it as such. But he had had no idea that it would stick in his mind like this and hurt a little too, deep down inside that he had not been taken into his son's confidence.

Mark had always felt very close to David, and he had great dreams for the boy's future. His son had always been at the head of his class in school; he was a tall, well-built, alert lad. He was quiet at home and had perhaps kept a little too much to himself, but Mark had never worried about that. David had a compulsive interest in outer space.

Mark could remember that night when the first missile circled the globe. Never had there been a more excited little boy than David. Wide-eyed, he had asked a million questions about the missile and when it would pass over the parsonage. He knew that people all over the world would be waiting eagerly and watching. The next morning David had been missing from his bed, but had been found a few minutes later asleep on a bench in the garden with a tall candle beside him. The candle had never been lit. The potential future astronaut had fallen asleep before the great event. He had missed seeing the missile because his sleepy self had to satisfy its demands, but it had taken little David a long time to get over that sorrow.

Mark realized now what a determined little fellow he had been from the very beginning of his life. Space, missiles, astronauts, moon travel, and now the possibility of travel to Mars had created for him a new world in which he had chosen to live. The rest of the world—home, parents, school, and friends—well, they were slowly becoming just a side issue, something that had to be recognized because it was already there.

The Reverend Mark Cartling sat at his desk in his spacious study in the educational wing of the church. His head was in his hands and he was deep in thought as he considered his Sunday sermon.

Perhaps he should change his topic. What should he preach on? What could he say? What words could he offer that would stir this new generation so that they would recognize that even in this scientific space age, they still had souls created by God and placed within them by Him, souls that had to be fed with spiritual food in order to grow, souls that were made to sparkle with joy, to lift and laugh and love. What text would suit them? Where was the magic formula?

Mark felt very tired and unable to cope with this great task, but he must reach his son and the rest of the young people. He must prove that being a preacher was something even more important than space travel. He must show them that the world needed not only more spacemen, but also more preachers who could deal with this age and give people the food they needed to develop into the great human race God had intended them to be from the beginning of time.

～ 4

MARK CARTLING sat on the wide top step of the church looking out over the peaceful valley below. He loved sitting here in the early morning; it gave him a sense of oneness with his church. The tall leafy trees hid all but a glimpse of blue ocean now, but when fall came and the trees shed their leaves, the ocean would seem nearer and wider. Although Mark could not see the church spire from where he was sitting, he was conscious of its existence. Like a beacon it called men to come, stop, and worship in the House of the Lord.

What a magnificent piece of architecture this building was, he thought. And what fantastic amounts of money had been spent to make it the plush church it was today. From the thick red carpeting on the sanctuary floor to the broad marble steps on which he was sitting, everything reflected wealth and abundance. Its landscaping was that of a miniature park with its many trees, bushes, and flowers artfully arranged.

Ever since that morning when Mark had overheard his son say that preachers and churches would soon be obsolete, he had assured himself that his position really was important. But every now and then he was haunted by the thought that David might possibly be right. Would there be a time when the Church would be a thing of the past? Would it, perhaps, be considered much the same as an antique—valued only as something beautiful from the past and kept for posterity as a reminder?

Something had to be done to establish the Church of God so firmly that nothing could ever undermine it. Mark wished he could contribute something to this cause, but he was all too aware of how powerless a minister could be in his own church. He attended to the preaching, called on the sick, comforted the bereaved, counseled the troubled, and welcomed newcomers in the community. Specifically his job was to welcome the wealthy in order to bring them in quickly for the benefit of the church. For the others, there was a membership committee. But the minister had nothing to do with the actual running of the church. The springs that kept the church overflowing with money were none of the minister's concern.

In this church there was a Mr. Rollins, a bank director, who had been Chairman of the Board of Directors of the church for years prior to Mark's arrival at Robendale-by-the-Sea. No one ever questioned Mr. Rollins' judgment. Perhaps no one dared question a man as wealthy and shrewd as he as long as the finances kept improving and a steady stream of money kept flowing into the coffers to keep up with the expenses of this large organization. Yes, Mark could see it so clearly this morning—he was the pastor, but Mr. Rollins ran the church. No matter what Mr. Rollins said, his word was law. He was, indeed, the supreme ruler. Mark had not thought too much about it until now. As he left the church step and walked across the grounds toward his study, a vision of Mr. Rollins' smooth, fat face seemed to accompany him.

As he entered the education building, he was met by the church secretary.

"Oh, there you are, Mr. Cartling," said Olive Loring with a smile. "There's a very insistent man on the telephone. I promised I would see if I could find you, and here you are."

"Thank you, Miss Loring. I'll take it in my study."

Mark hurried into the study and picked up the phone. On the line was a Mr. Johnson from the Town Planning Board. He asked for an early appointment, which was set for a half hour later. It always pleased Mark to be included in the planning for the town, and he found he was often consulted about things in the community.

Mr. Johnson arrived exactly on time. As far as Mark knew, this man was not a member of any church in town. He was a tall thin individual with hands that twitched nervously as he talked in a crisp monotone. He seated himself opposite Mark's large desk and came right to the point.

"We need your help, Mr. Cartling. There seems to be some opposition from the board of your church about the demolition of some deathtrap apartments in the north end of town. I'm confident that you can clear this up for us. You see, fires have been plentiful there lately, and the lack of sanitation is beyond human decency for these progressive times."

Mark smiled a wide friendly smile.

"I'd be happy to help you in any way I can, Mr. Johnson. I have no idea why there should be any opposition here. As I recall, none of my flock even lives down there."

"No. I'm quite sure of that, Mr. Cartling, and the opposition doesn't come from a tenement dweller. I've already talked to the chairman of your church board. I went to him first so that I wouldn't have to bother you with business matters. But your man wouldn't budge, even when I explained that we needed that property to build a swimming pool for the many underprivileged children so badly in need of a recreation area. Now wouldn't you think that a project like that would find help from a church, especially one as important as the Community Church?"

Mark laughed.

"It seems to me that it is a most worthy cause, Mr. Johnson, but I'm a bit puzzled as to what our church has to do with it."

Mr. Johnson's burning eyes stared at Mark's face in unbelief.

"Are my ears deceiving me, or are you really unaware

of what I'm getting at? It certainly has never been a secret that your Community Church has held the deeds on those apartments for years and that your business of saving souls thrives on the dirt and squalor of those tenants."

Mark stood up. He felt his face flush with embarrassment and anger. Mr. Johnson arose, too, and the two men faced each other.

Mr. Johnson's last words had really been a deliberate, vengeful sneer. He continued in a gentler tone, "I had hoped I wouldn't have to say that, Mr. Cartling, but your coyness forced me to do so. This is precisely why I never joined any church. They're all profit-making organizations. Some people are forever getting rich at the expense of the poor. Well, I'm leaving it up to you now. I'll give you thirty days, Mr. Cartling, and in that time I hope you can convert your Mr. Rollins. We have to have his signature before we can send a wrecking crew in there, and the people have to have time to pack and get moved. By that time, those new low-cost apartments down by the river will be ready for occupancy. Now it's in your hands. Good day, Mr. Cartling, and thank you for your time."

Long after the door had closed behind Mr. Johnson, Mark sat staring at his desk. A numbness filled him. He could not believe what he had heard. How could Mr. Rollins make such use of money given by people in good faith? How could he invest it in filth and dirt, in faulty housing, supporting a sore spot in the community? And all the while the capital was safely stored away in Mr.

Rollins' bank. He was a hard-core businessman all right, with not an ounce of charity in him.

After awhile Mark pulled himself together and his fingers mechanically dialed the number of the most influential bank in town. His voice was hoarse and tense as he asked to speak to Mr. Rollins, and a few seconds later, the jovial, deep voice reached his ear.

"Well, good morning, Pastor! Thanks for the pleasant time Mrs. Rollins and I enjoyed at the parsonage the other evening. I don't know when we've had such a good time. When we got home I said to Helen that we're not only blessed with one of the finest preachers in this part of the country, but also one of the loveliest hostesses who ever graced a parsonage."

"Thank you, Mr. Rollins. I'm glad you enjoyed yourselves; so did my family. Nothing like sharing your home with church members! . . . But I'm calling because something important has come up—something that has me quite upset. I'd like very much to meet with you as soon as possible. Is there a chance to make it today?"

"Of course! Let's meet at the Country Club for lunch. Would one o'clock suit you? . . . Oh, I won't take no for an answer. We'll meet in the lobby. See you then."

The phone clicked in Mark's ear.

Just like that, thought Mark. Mr. Rollins always kills people with kindness. Well, Mark would be there, but he thoroughly intended to have more than lunch. They must have a long talk and he had to change that man's mind. The church funds had to be withdrawn from that slum housing. Somehow he must find the right words.

"Will you have a drink to simmer you down a little, Pastor? . . . Oh, don't give me that look now. I should have known better than to ask you, but one wouldn't hurt. I'm not a drinker, but I need one before a meal to take the edge off the day's tension which seems to have imposed itself on the church as well. Times have changed, I guess, and so has the church. There are no saints there any more. . . . You'll excuse me if I go ahead and have mine?"

It didn't take long for Mark to get to the subject of the apartments, and while they were eating, he did most of the talking. Mr. Rollins seemed to listen quietly without much comment.

"Are those the facts, Mr. Rollins?" asked Mark. "And if they are, who has given you the authority to invest church money in such unworthy projects? It's not just unworthy, it's harmful and it's bringing the scorn of the whole town upon the church."

Mr. Rollins laughed heartily.

"At times, Mark Cartling, you remind me of a little boy just out of school. The church has left the responsibility for its investments up to me. It's my business and I'm always looking for the ones that bring the most benefit. Why do you think our church is one of the wealthiest churches in New England, debt free, paying enormous salaries to its ministers and educators, and maintaining an extremely expensive parsonage for its senior minister? Money doesn't grow on trees, but it does grow if you know where to plant it.

"The preaching, Pastor, the salvation of souls, the visitation and the membership—I never intrude on these, and I ask the same courtesy from you regarding my position. I know what I'm doing and those apartments have brought us a pretty penny every year. They aren't too bad for people who can't afford to pay a decent rent. Most of the occupants are drunks and misfits anyway. Those people don't want their housing torn down. They don't care if their children have a swimming pool. All they want is a roof over their heads, and they know we aren't too hard on them if they get a few months behind on their rent. But they also know they have to pay sometime or out they go. I don't have too much trouble collecting from them. It's a good deal for them. So in a way, we're helping them whether you can see it or not."

Mark waited patiently until Mr. Rollins finished his speech. Then he spoke in a voice mingled with pain and frustration.

"I had no idea that anything like this could go on in a Christian church. We are a church, you know, not a business! I'm shocked to think that the Town Planning Board had to come to ask us to be charitable and decent enough to help keep up the progress of our times. I thought the ministers and church members worked together for the glory of the Kingdom of God. I was proud of our church. I had lofty dreams for her. How can I go on living in an expensive parsonage, knowing that those people are living in dirt and rubble to pay for my luxury and comfort? Are you the only one who can decide on this, Mr. Rollins?"

"Fortunately, yes. A unanimous vote by the Board about ten years ago finalized that, and the former pastor was the one who suggested it. But let's not have unpleasant words about it. I might be a blunt fool at times, but I have a heart, too. I like peace, and I like having an agreeable relationship between the church board and the minister. If you'd like, I'll show you the figures later on. We'll go over the whole thing. You said we had a month. Well, before the month is up, I'm sure you'll see all this my way. Those people would be lost in a clean neighborhood."

And so would you, Mr. Rollins, thought Mark, after he had said good-bye to the bank director. His heart was pounding hard as he climbed into his car and drove north through the business section down toward the river. It was easy to find the apartments in question. They stood gray and sullen against the hot summer sky. Dogs and cats looked for something edible in coverless garbage cans. The grassless lawn areas were littered with papers and empty beer bottles. A few children were digging in the hot sand—their faces dirty and lifeless.

Mark parked his car and entered the vestibule of one of the buildings. The walls were unpainted and the plaster was falling from the ceiling. He scanned some of the mail boxes for names and picked out one—Albert D. Hyland.

He pressed the bell, but there was no sound. He rapped on the door, but no one came to open it. Mark turned the knob and opened the door. On the other side was a dark, dingy hall, but he managed to find the name Hyland on the door to the left. He knocked and heard footsteps coming. The door opened just a crack, and a woman's pale face peered out.

"We don't want to buy anything," she said curtly, ready to shut the door again.

But Mark spoke up quickly. "I'm Mr. Cartling, the pastor of the Community Church on the hill. May I come in and talk with you for a moment?"

"Are you a priest?" Her eyes widened, and she opened the door enough for Mark to enter. "We're not used to having callers like you."

"I'm not a priest. I'm of the Protestant faith, madam, but I'm making a friendly house call. Does it matter?"

"Goodness, no! Come in! But we have no money to give to your church. We're Catholics, but I haven't been inside a church for five years, may the Lord have mercy on my soul."

Mark glanced around the room. It was shabby, but fairly clean. The white curtains at the windows had seen better days. He noticed the torn wallpaper and that the plaster was almost gone from the ceiling.

"Excuse the looks of things. We can't get anything repaired and we haven't the money to pay for it ourselves. Things seem to go from bad to worse, year after year. My husband Albert is in the hospital, and it's lucky for me and the children that we can stay here. We're three months behind on the rent now. I do housework three times a week, but this week I was laid off my best-paying job. I'm too tired and I don't work fast enough any more. Too much trouble. It wears on you, but we'll try to get along somehow. If only Albert recovers and goes back to work. I'm glad you came. It was nice of you to call."

Mark was relieved that she had kept up the steady stream of conversation. It had given him time to collect his thoughts and to try to rid himself of the lump in his throat.

"I'll be glad to call on your husband," offered Mark. "What is his hospital room number?"

The woman laughed. "He has no number. He's in the ward of the municipal hospital."

Mark sat down and talked a while longer with Mrs. Hyland. When he was saying good-bye, he slipped a ten-dollar bill into her hand.

"Just a little something to tide you over," he said. "I'll see your husband and I'll be back to talk with you again soon."

Mrs. Hyland's eyes glistened with fresh tears. She wiped them off with the back of her hand. Her eyes thanked Mark more than her words. Never had he seen more gratitude in a woman's face.

It felt good to get into the fresh air again, but something within him seemed to want to explode. What a pathetic way for the church to make money, he thought. What a brilliant testimony this was for a wealthy church with all its charities and missions. The shame of it seemed more than Mark could bear.

He was too upset to return to his study. He decided to go home. He would sit in the parsonage garden and soak up the sun and the beauty of trees and flowers. He had to have stillness to think.

He hoped that Elsa was home so he could talk this over with her. She would know what to do. Elsa always knew.

~ 5

THREE WEEKS had passed since that afternoon when Mark had gone home to talk to Elsa. He had found her on her hands and knees in the rock garden, weeding and scratching among the flowers and plants near the bird-bath. He had paused for a moment to watch her. What a picture she had made in her red pants and white shirt, sleeves rolled up for work, and a red ribbon in her blonde hair! She looked like a schoolgirl.

"Hi!" he had called as he strolled across the lawn.

She had looked up, giving him a big smile, glowing with warmth and love.

"Hi, yourself," she had called back. "What brings you home this early on a working day?"

"Just homesickness, I guess! It's such a hot day that I thought I'd spend some time in our garden."

Elsa had risen to meet him, taking his arm, leading him to a comfortable lounge chair. Mark had stretched out and it had felt good. He had not realized just how tired he was until that moment.

41

"I'll get some cool drinks," Elsa had offered, heading for the back door. "You wouldn't believe this, Mark, but for some strange reason I made your favorite brownies this morning."

A bit of Elsa's gaiety had rubbed off. Mark had never seen her as happy as she seemed to be in this parsonage. How could he tell her about his unpleasant discovery— that this church with all its zeal and glamour carried a malignancy beneath its beauty, that all was not well with its foundation, that it could not go forward to God's glory in its present condition, and that if he tried to put the knife to the evil, he might lose his job? No, he couldn't discuss this with Elsa today. He must let her be happy for as long as it lasted. If the worst happened, there would be time enough to tell her about Mr. Rollins' power. He would try to forget it for the present and just enjoy this afternoon in the garden in her gay company. It was easy to dispel the gloom as they sat together sipping lemonade from tall frosty glasses and munching on the delicious brownies. If there was one thing that Elsa could bake to perfection, it was brownies.

It seemed to Mark that his wife could converse fluently on almost any subject she chose, and that afternoon it was the parsonage garden.

"You know, Mark," she had said, "the family who lived here before us must have loved this garden. I've never seen so many growing things. Every day there are more surprises with new things popping out of the ground."

42

"Perhaps they knew your secret, Elsa. Perhaps they talked to the trees and flowers just as you do."

"I'm sure they did just that, Mark. They must have loved every single thing in this garden. You can always tell when a garden has been loved; everything blossoms so much better."

"Well, you'd better keep up the loving and talking, Elsa. In the long run, it should save a lot on the fertilizer bill."

"You know that has nothing to do with it. Even plants with love have to have food . . . oh, Mark, you're teasing me."

Mark had laughed aloud at Elsa's mock grimace. It had turned out to be a very pleasant afternoon. It had been cool under the shade of the trees and only the birds singing in the treetops had broken the solitude.

But this morning was hot and humid, as Mark sat at his desk in the church study, thinking back on the last three weeks. He had, in that time, disciplined his own life to reaffirm his desire to be a useful servant for his Master. He knew he could not compromise and he knew, also, that his church must become involved with the problems of the world. He felt a need to teach each member what it meant to be a soldier in God's army— to fight sin and corruption, to lift the fallen, and to let the defeated know that love could heal and restore them. But before the church could reach out into the world, it first had to reach up and receive the power promised to those who belonged to the Kingdom of

43

God. To prepare himself for delivering this lesson, Mark had elected to rise each morning at five-thirty, before the busy life of the ministry began, to leave the parsonage and walk up the hill to the church. There he fasted until noon. This he had vowed to continue until he found a solution to the apartment problem.

Although he spent these hours in prayerful meditation and self-searching, he found it difficult to pray for Mr. Rollins. In his heart he almost hated that man. Several times they had met to discuss a possible answer to give Mr. Johnson when he returned, but Rollins always evaded the real issue, tossing off Mark's proposals with a joke. Yes, James H. Rollins was the biggest stumbling block in Mark's path just now.

Mr. Rollins had made it quite clear that if a choice arose between Mark and the apartments, Mark would be the one to go.

"Hold it," Rollins had burst out during one heated conversation. "Who do you think you are? I want you to know that this church can afford to buy its ministers and I must remind you again that the Board, not the minister, runs the church. You have your job to do, and if you know what's best for you, you'd better stick to it."

Mark had tried to remain composed, but his throat was dry and his words clipped.

"As a minister I am the shepherd of my flock, and it is my responsibility before God to see that they follow the right path."

Rollins stared at Mark, his eyes angry, and his words spilled out like hot lava.

44

"I'm disappointed in you, Cartling—you and your so-called ideals. When we called you to this church, we thought you were a peace-loving man. Your former church was small and insignificant, and we were sure that you would appreciate a more-than-adequate salary and a very comfortable parsonage. As a speaker you are superior. There are more people attending services now than we can take care of. But that does not give you the right to interfere in money matters. I am in charge there and you are merely a tool in my hand. If that tool becomes no longer useful, I'll discard it. And if you don't think I mean it, just try me."

With that Mr. Rollins left abruptly, slamming the door behind him. Mark could never remember having felt so angry and insulted. So that was their reason for calling him, because they thought he would be blind to their sins for a sum. It was a bribe! What a mockery they were making of a servant of God.

Mark expected a visit from some of the Board members in the following days, but no one came. And the next time they met, James Rollins was his old jovial self. Mark had never before dealt with such a man. He was as slippery as an eel, and there seemed to be no way to catch him. But there must be a way....

This morning Mark felt sorry for Mr. Rollins. Here was a man in great need of help. He needed it almost more than those people in the north end. I must remember that, Mark thought. It would be a challenge—to guide this stubborn man into the love of God.

Where did a minister's work end? Everywhere hands

were reaching out for help and voices were asking for advice. At times the weight of his work was almost too heavy, and finding the lost keys to so many problems took so much time.

Mark opened the big Bible on his desk, turning to a familiar passage underlined in red. It was the fortieth chapter of the prophet Isaiah, the thirty-first verse. He read it aloud, slowly and distinctly, as though he wanted to imprint each precious word on his mind:

> "But they that wait upon the Lord shall renew their strength; they shall mount up with wings as eagles; they shall run, and not be weary; and they shall walk, and not faint."

Bright sunshine flooded the room. It shone down on the thick teal-blue carpet and enriched the oil paintings on the walls. It glowed warmly on the massive, hand-carved black walnut desk and a few rays even strayed to Mark's folded hands, white and motionless. It was as if those rays were making an unsuccessful attempt to penetrate the darkness of Mark's confused thought world.

Mark suffered for the shame of his church, its sacred purpose to help and heal the world defiled. How different his former church had been. There his opinion had been respected. Those dear people knew that the Gospel he proclaimed was real and relevant and that the church was a light in the community, the tender of which was the minister. Those people did not buy their minister; they called him to do the will of God. This was not the first time that Mark found himself regretting his present job. What had it given him but heartache? Was that the price he had to pay for falling for the temptation of fame, wealth, and beauty? Well, the act was done and Mark had no intention of retreating until his work was completed. He must pray, trusting that he would find a way to do his job and do it well.

Sitting there Mark let his mind wander back through the years. He was a boy of thirteen again, living with his parents and sister on a small farm in Maine. His father was a potato farmer and his property lay on the outskirts of a small village whose only recreation for its youth was the church and a movie theater. It was an unattractive and isolated community, but Mark had never been lonely. There was a warm closeness in his home, and although he had many chores to do after school, he still had plenty of time to wander. Mark had loved the miles and miles of untouched woodland and he spent much time just tramping through the woods. At times he would sit motionless on a stone, just waiting. And if he waited long enough, he was rewarded. The birds would begin to sing, perching very near to him. The rabbits hopped around without fear and on occasion a woodchuck or fox came stepping through the brambles. Sometimes, to his delight, deer would venture forth from the shadows and graze silently only yards away. These were golden moments when Mark felt at one with God's wonderful world.

On one of those days, as Mark wandered through the

woods, he stumbled upon a strange rock, different from any he had ever seen. It was large, almost mountainous to a small boy, and it seemed to jut out in all directions. But its top was flat. From the top Mark had a wide view of the world around him. He could see the distant mountains rising high, blue and majestic. And the spruces with their pointed tops, so straight and tall, gave off a delicate fragrance on that warm summer day. It was a friendly world, full of wonder and mystery, and the rock was a friendly rock, not made of stone, but with a heart and ears. Mark called it "his rock" and whenever he went into the woods, he always returned to it. There he pondered life and eternity. There he had made his decision to enter the ministry to proclaim to the world a God who had created a beautiful world. He would even stand on the rock and make up sermons. It had thrilled him to hear his own voice calling out into the wilderness. How strong and convincing, bold and demanding, or soft and pleading he could make it! The rock became a part of his life.

This morning Mark wondered if the rock was still there, or if it had been leveled to make room for a highway. It had been so long since he had visited Maine. His father had died suddenly; and after Mark had left home the farm had been sold; his mother had made her home with his married sister outside of Boston. At the moment he had a strange longing to go back. If only he could sit on that rock again, lifting up his heart to God in trust and simplicity, he might find the solution to his problem. At one time Mark had thought he would

48

like to show David the little farm and the rock, but now he feared that David would laugh at the rock as he had at the ministry. A boy of this space age, so steeped in mathematics and science, would certainly think his father naïve to be so sentimental over a rock. No, David would never understand. There was a gap between them even though Mark wanted so much to be close to his son. Once he had had a dream that David would follow in his footsteps; now that dream was dead. . . . But there was still little Eric to build his hope on. Eric was a loving, dependable little boy with very important problems on his mind. But at least he still confided in his father.

Just the other night, after a quick game of horseshoes, as they walked back toward the parsonage in the semi-darkness, Eric had slipped his hand into his father's.

"Eric," Mark had said, "what ever happened to that dog you wanted? Have you stopped thinking about it?"

"Yeah! I can't have a dog following me around and be in Bernie's house most of the time. Mrs. Danewich doesn't like dogs. Guess her stuff is too fancy. But there's something else I want, Dad. I want it very much."

"And what is that, Eric?"

"I want to be a Jew, Dad! I want to be a Jew like Bernie and go to the synagogue."

Mark, taken by surprise, had a great impulse to laugh at the irony of it all, but because Eric was so serious, he had controlled his voice and said, "Eric, you must understand, Bernie was born a Jew. Being Jewish is part of his heritage."

"Well, then," said Eric, "I suppose that's out for me!"

Mark had wanted to reason some more with him, but they had entered the parsonage, found dinner awaiting them and the conversation was lost.

Children of today were different. They were so restless and wanted such strange things. There was Susan, compromising her faith with Gary. She had, perhaps, had many talks with Father Smith. Mark could not bring himself to ask her. But Gary had counseled with Mark several times. Why were today's young people not safe and secure in their own faith as Mark had been when he was growing up? There were so many why's.

But Mark had to put his thoughts away. A new day had begun. Mr. Johnson would return before long and he would have to be told something definite. But for today Mark looked over his schedule. There were members he must call on—a few needed counseling; some were in the hospital. There were some committees to meet with and he had to speak at the Rotary Club at noon. In the afternoon he would call on more people in the apartments. He wanted to know them all. That would be a beginning anyway.

The intercom buzzed. It was Miss Loring.

"There is a young couple here to see you, Mr. Cartling."

"Send them in, please."

And the day's work had begun. Mark looked again at his Bible, then closed it gently and put it away.

"They shall mount up with wings as eagles . . ."

~ 6

ELSA HAD NEVER been happier in all her life than here in this parsonage. She awoke every morning with a feeling of joyous anticipation. Coming downstairs to her pretty modern kitchen to start breakfast for the children was a happy chore, a task she looked forward to performing. The children usually came straggling down one by one, sleepy-eyed, but dressed and ready for school. Mark rarely had breakfast with the family, since he left in the early hours for his study. So Elsa was alone with her children in the morning and very often from their conversations, she learned what was on their young minds. Each day they had a brief period of devotion which the youngsters themselves conducted, each choosing a Bible reading and the topic he wanted to discuss. This, Elsa felt, was a tie binding them closer together in a world where everything seemed to be scattered about.

Here at Robendale-by-the-Sea Elsa had more time

to herself than she had had in any other of Mark's parishes. Here her duties seemed to consist of being sweet and charming, of sitting beside her husband at the head table at church functions, and of giving some time to social and civic organizations whenever she was asked. These she performed willingly. When a request came, Elsa sought to represent her church in the best way.

How different it had been in those former churches. There she had had to fill in everywhere and was often called upon to be a personal counselor when Mark was out of town. At such times she was expected to try to fill Mark's shoes. Sometimes it had been thrilling, and at other times frightening, but always she had felt a deep sense of satisfaction that she was trying to understand her husband's great challenge.

Then, when Mark returned, she had always felt a great sense of relief. He could take over the reins again and she could retreat to her job as housekeeper and mother to three lively children.

On those nights, after the children were tucked in bed, Elsa and Mark used to sit down to talk things over and she would relate the happenings of the busy day. Sometimes in the fall, when the wind blowing outside made the house creak and groan, they would have a fire in the fireplace, leaving the lights low, to create that certain coziness that belonged to home.

"I'm so glad you're back, dear," she would begin. "What a day this has been! Sometimes I think people make up troubles to keep their handsome pastor hopping."

"Shame on you, Elsa," Mark would tease. "You know

52

this only happens when I am away. What they really want is to come inside the parsonage and be comforted and coddled by the inexperienced half of this ministry."

"The way you take off, it won't be long before I really am experienced."

"Well, let me have it! What happened to my sheep today?"

"First there was Mrs. Harris. If that Ida isn't a dilly, I don't know who is. She was having mother-in-law trouble again."

"It happens too often and her mother-in-law isn't easy to take. We all know that."

"Well, today Ida was in tears because Larry had given the tenderloin of last night's steak to his mother and she had received the tough tail end. That's what I was supposed to settle."

"And I'll bet you did!"

Elsa smiled. "Poor Ida is so excitable, but I managed to calm her. I convinced her that Larry had done what he did only because his mother has such poor teeth that the only way she could eat steak was to have it tender. I told Ida she should be glad she was blessed with beautiful, strong teeth that could chew the toughest meat."

"How clever of you, Elsa."

"Ida seemed to think it over and she said I probably was right. It was hard for her mother-in-law to chew meat. She decided that she had been picky and selfish and she would try to turn over another leaf and be more thoughtful of Larry's sickly mother."

"I think I'll make you the church office counselor."

"Then my first counsel would be for the pastor of this church to set Larry Harris straight. His wife needs a lot more consideration."

"I'll make a mental note of that. . . . What else happened?"

"Mrs. Dorset called. Her husband was in trouble and she needed to get hold of you in the worst way. When I told her you were out of town, she almost went out of her mind. Finally she came over here and blurted out the whole story. Albert Dorset had written another bad check. Of course he couldn't be found, but the bank had given Mrs. Dorset twenty-four hours to cover it or Albert would be arrested. Luckily it was only twenty-five dollars, but she had no way to raise the money."

"So you gave it to her."

"How did you know?"

"Because I know my Elsa. There goes your new suit."

"Oh, well, my old one is still in pretty good shape, and, Mark, we couldn't let Albert Dorset give a bad name to his church."

Mark would hug her then and Elsa soon forgot her problem day.

"You are very, very special, Mrs. Cartling," he would say tenderly. "Have I ever told you that?"

It was wonderful to know that Mark was pleased. It made up for all the work, so she would decide not to tell him about Mrs. Robinson and her teen-age daughter, or about the Sunday-school teacher who was quitting because the Superintendent was playing favorites. All that could wait. She would just relax and know that

54

the two of them were a team, working together for the good of mankind.

But here, in Robendale, Mark did not need her help. The church was so well staffed that there was a committee to handle any problem. Even though Elsa missed her close association with her husband, she would never tell him how she felt. Perhaps, she thought, people in this community didn't have as many troubles and heartaches as the people with whom they had worked before.

But the previous night something had come up in which Elsa felt she could participate. At the dinner table Mark had spoken of a young couple he was to marry the next day. He said that he felt sorry for the prospective bride. She seemed so young and sweet and there had been tears in her eyes when she confided to Mark that she had always dreamt of a big wedding with flowers and candles and guests and of a large reception. Now all she was going to have was a church-study ceremony.

"But, Mark," Elsa had said, "why didn't you suggest that they be married in the parsonage. Let me fuss a little for them. You know I'd love to plan a wedding here."

"I don't think we should start anything like that," said Mark. "This isn't New Hampshire, Elsa. People here are sophisticated and the Board wouldn't like it."

"Oh, hang the Board!" said Elsa laughing. "I think those young people deserve a nice wedding. Let me do it just this once, Mark."

Mark wavered, and Elsa kept on.

"Just this once, Mark. The Board need never know about it, and I'm sure we'd make two young people very happy."

"I'll let you do it on one condition, Elsa, that you never again ask to do such a thing."

"That's a promise. But this time, let me fuss."

And so it was settled. Mark was to bring the young people to the parsonage and Elsa free to do her planning, could hardly wait until the following day.

The wedding day was Irma's day at the parsonage, so Elsa had help. And Irma was equally excited about the wedding. She baked the wedding cake, which Elsa decorated with white bells, pale pink roses, and tiny green leaves. In addition, there would be filled sandwich rolls, pickles, olives, potato chips, and a special ice cream to go with the cake. There was a lovely bouquet of pink roses in a silver bowl in the center of the dining-room table on which Elsa had set out wedding napkins and little favors. There were ten places at the table because Elsa had managed to find some guests to attend the ceremony. Susan had assured her that she could get Gary to come, and Eric had volunteered Bernie and his mother. With the bridal couple, Mark, Elsa, and Irma, every place would be filled.

The wedding was to take place in the family room, which was flooded with sunshine in the late afternoon. Irma had put up wedding bells, both large and small, and there was a large palm in one corner and a beautiful fern, which was Elsa's pride. And there were flowers everywhere. Elsa had almost stripped the parsonage

56

gardens, knowing there would be more blooms soon. This was to be such a special occasion that everything had to be beautiful. Susan had promised to play the wedding march, and Elsa was glad that the piano was in the family room and that Susan played so well. Everything was fine except for David. He had declined his invitation to attend.

"I think it's perfectly disgusting to have a wedding party for a couple you don't even know. Count me out! I don't want any part of it."

And Elsa had to let it go at that, knowing he would be shut up down in the basement. Nothing could lure him away from his laboratory and his invention.

At four o'clock everything was in order. Elsa and Irma sat down to relax and behold their art work. They both agreed that it couldn't be more beautiful.

"It's been such fun!" said Elsa, feeling content and happy.

"You certainly are wonderful to go to all this work and expense for a couple of strangers. I do hope they appreciate it."

"I'm sure they will, Irma. It might be crazy to do things like this, but I get such a kick out of it. And I'd better enjoy it now, because I promised Mr. Cartling I wouldn't ask to do it again. He wasn't very enthused about the whole idea."

"Well, men are different when it comes to weddings, but I'm sure he'll be pleased when he sees what a perfect party it is."

"I hope so. You know, Irma, my husband is not as

carefree as he used to be. He's so proper about everything in this town. I wish you could have known him the way he was before."

"Perhaps this big church it too much for him," suggested Irma.

"No, I don't think that's it. It always takes time to get used to a new church. The first year is usually the honeymoon; but when the second year comes along, the pastor really begins to know his people and the demands begin to pile up. In another year, Mr. Cartling will be himself again."

The doorbell chimed and the guests arrived. Irma had just time to guide them into the family room when Mark and the bridal couple arrived. Mark introduced them to Elsa.

"Elsa, this is Betsy Hall and Karl Strouth. Betsy and Karl, this is my wife, Mrs. Cartling."

Betsy took Elsa's hand.

"Mrs. Cartling, we are delighted to be here. I've never heard of a minister's wife being so kind and generous. We are grateful."

"It's been fun!" said Elsa, smiling and thinking to herself how very young the bride and groom looked.

Mark slipped on his black robe, and Susan began to play softly. At the right time, she began the Wedding March, and Betsy and Karl, hand in hand, walked toward Mark, taking each step slowly, knowing it was only a short distance to the preacher. The music stopped and Susan sat down beside Gary. The room was very still. Mark looked very tall and dignified holding his

58

small black book. His voice was firm but mellow as he began the old ceremony he had read so many times before. Finally he came to the all important questions.

"Do you, Karl, take this woman to be your lawfully wedded wife. . ."

Karl's "I do" was loud and clear.

Then Mark turned to Betsy.

"Do you, Betsy, take this man——"

But Mark never had a chance to finish. A strange odor filled the room followed by a loud explosion. The palm crashed to the floor, and the floorboards creaked and splintered. The lovely carpet split right on the spot where Betsy was standing, throwing her into Elsa's beautiful fern. Mrs. Danewich cradled both Eric and Bernie in her arms; her face was ashen. Elsa felt dazed, as if she were not a part of the whole scene. Then she shuddered as she looked at Mark's pale face. Quite suddenly, in the silence of the aftermath, the prospective bride dropped to her knees, sobbing uncontrollably. Karl tried to comfort her, but she seemed unaware of his presence. Her face was smeared with dirt and tears, and her hands were clasped tightly, her eyes closed. At first she seemed to be moaning; then Elsa realized she was praying.

"Dear Lord," she cried, "please don't let the world end. It's all my fault. I know Mother begged me not to get married. If only You will give me another chance, I promise to wait. Please . . . please . . ."

"Betsy," said Mark breathlessly, "the world is not ending. That was just an explosion in the basement. The hot water heater must have blown up. Now calm down so I can investigate. I'll be right back to finish your ceremony."

Mark turned abruptly and hurried down the basement steps. In her heart Elsa knew it was not the hot water heater. She knew that just under the family room was David's laboratory, and she grew hot and cold at the same time. If only she could have followed Mark . . . but she had to stay with the guests while horrible thoughts crossed her mind.

Could David have had explosives in his workshop? If he had, they could all have been killed! Was David hurt himself? . . . What was the matter with this generation? They did what they wanted to do regardless of the consequences.

Elsa felt tears near, but she knew she had to appear calm. She forced a smile just for those darling kids who had had their wedding spoiled—the bride almost scared to death—they must never know how upset she was. Soon Mark would be back to explain. She strained to hear what was going on a flight below, but all she could hear were loud voices, then hurried steps heading outside. As she went to the window she saw Mark and David drive off. Where was Mark taking David?

Elsa held back the tears and tried to compose herself.

"We will know what happened as soon as Pastor Cartling returns," she said. "Something must have happened to David. Mark took him off in the car."

"Mrs. Cartling," said Betsy, the tears still running down her cheeks, "we won't have to wait. We aren't getting married. This was meant to happen. I'm sure

60

the explosion was an accident, but it did knock some sense into my head. You see, we can have a beautiful church wedding if we wait. My parents want to give me the very best, but they don't want us to get married now. They like Karl, but they want him to finish college first and get a job. But we wouldn't listen. We wanted to get married right away. Adults don't know how long a few years can seem to young people in love. Just a few minutes ago I thought the world was ending. I've never been so scared. But it was good for me, because now I can wait as long as I have to and I hope Karl will wait for me."

Karl took her hand. "I don't want to, but I will, Betsy. It was awful to hear you pleading with God. I guess the wedding is off, for now."

"But not the party," said Elsa. "Let's sit down and have some refreshments while we wait for my husband. This will be the first time I've eaten a wedding cake for a bride who didn't get married."

But the gaiety had vanished as they sat down at the table—a crestfallen groom and a still-tearful bride. And the conversation dragged, even though everyone made a valiant effort to keep it going.

"It's such a shame," said Mrs. Danewich. "Everything began so perfectly and the room looked so beautiful."

"I thought it was an earthquake," said Bernie.

"Even I was scared," admitted Eric. "But then I began to figure that it must be David. He had lots of explosives down in his lab. I guess something just blew up."

"Yes," agreed Elsa, now that Eric had voiced her own

61

thoughts, "it must have been David. But we'll know for sure when your dad returns."

Then Elsa turned to Betsy with a smile. "You see, we have an older son who experiments and invents as a hobby. But I assure you, if he had explosives down there in the basement, I knew nothing about it. I would never have believed that he would bring anything as dangerous as explosives into the parsonage without permission, which we, of course, would never have given. I am so terribly sorry. Please forgive David for causing all this trouble, which I'm pretty sure he did."

"When we get married," said Gary, "I'm going to be sure that David is the best man so he can't spoil the wedding."

Irma didn't say anything. She looked stunned by what had happened. But her eyes seemed to tell Elsa how badly she felt for her and her lovely party.

It was a whole hour before Mark returned. Elsa met him at the door and told him of the strange change of plans. Solemnly Mark tried to explain what had happened. It was David's experiment, not the water heater, that had caused the explosion. Mark was furious.

"I'm appalled," he stormed, "to think that our son, who is almost seventeen years old, could do such a thing. He knows you can't have explosives in a private house. Then to ignite something near them! I wish you could have seen him. He burned the seat out of his pants and just barely escaped being badly burned. But he'll be considerably uncomfortable for quite a while. He'll be in the hospital for a few days. I hope you all

62

understand why I had to rush off. I'm so embarrassed and ashamed; I don't know how to make amends for our guests' inconvenience."

"Did anything catch fire in the basement?" asked Susan.

"No, luckily David was able to extinguish the fire right away, so only the carpet burned a little. The floor is concrete, which helped."

"He isn't badly hurt then?" asked Elsa anxiously.

"No. His burns will be somewhat painful, and then there is the shock of what happened. But the worst thing to him is that his invention blew up. That almost killed him. He cried like a baby over that. David claims it will take years to rebuild what he lost. That's what really seemed to bother him."

"I am sure he's sorry," said Elsa shakily. "David wouldn't have wanted to cause all this commotion and upset the wedding. I want to apologize for my son."

"Don't worry about it at all, Mrs. Cartling," said Betsy, who was now able to smile again. "It happened for a reason. It was supposed to happen. David isn't really to blame."

But Elsa still had to fight back the tears that wanted to come. How could she ever trust David again? . . . Yet she was thankful it had not turned out worse.

That day was one of the strangest that Elsa could ever remember. Her heart ached for David. She knew Mark would be severe with him when he returned from the hospital and that his experimenting would have to stop for a while. She worried about how it would effect her son. Mark planned to have a carpenter fix the floorboards and a rug man repair the carpet so the trustees of the church would not know about the incident. She felt she could not collect from the church this time, this expense the Cartlings would bear. The only good seemed to be that two youngsters had not been married. Elsa wondered if a Higher Power had been behind it all. She would never forget this day and how lovely the parsonage had looked and how she and Irma had fussed for the wedding. She guessed that parsonages were places where almost anything could happen. Life there was certainly not monotonous.

A few days later, when a note came from Betsy, Elsa was sure the whole event had taken place for a reason, and a warm feeling filled her as she read:

Dear Reverend and Mrs. Cartling,

How can we ever thank you for all your kindness? Karl and I know now that it is right for us to wait. I told Mother what happened and she is grateful, too. Someday, I am sure, you will meet her as we all hope that when the happy day arrives, you—Reverend Cartling—will come and finish what you began. Please don't say no.

Thank you again from the bottom of my heart.

With love,
Betsy Hall

Elsa held the letter in her hand a long time, as she relived those awful moments of that strange day. As a mother, she knew how happy Betsy's mother must feel

64

at her daughter's decision. Perhaps the experience had also been good for Gary and Susan. They certainly would never forget that sobbing prayer from the bride's heart. Maybe it would make them think more deeply before they planned their own wedding, so that when the day came, it would be one of beauty and happiness.

~ 7

THE MOMENT Mark opened his eyes he knew it had all been a dream. But never before had he experienced a dream that had seemed so real. Could it have been a vision? he wondered. Did God still send visions in dream form as he had in Biblical times? If so, this might just be an answer to prayer, and he would treat it as such. In any case, it had solved the most pressing problem of today, his meeting with Mr. Johnson of the Town Planning Board. Mark glanced at the clock on the bedside table. It was 5:30 A.M. He was too wide awake to go back to sleep, so he began to go over the dream again, trying to visualize the events just as they had come to him.

It had been one of those nights when Mark had been too tired mentally to go to sleep immediately. He was troubled about his coming meeting with Mr. Johnson, since he had nothing constructive to report.

Then there was the problem of David. It hurt Mark

66

to think of his tall, handsome, elder son. Since that accident in the basement, David had slumped into a mood of depression, and Mark knew it was because of the padlock on his laboratory door. There had been a stormy session in the parsonage when Mark had ruled that there would be no more explosives in the basement or anywhere else in the house and that David would have to find another interest. The look in David's dark eyes had said more than the resentment in his words.

"You don't get it, Dad! You want to cut me off! It doesn't matter to you what I want to do. A few cracked boards mean more to you than your own son."

Mark had tried to calm him down.

"It's only for a time, David. I assure you, I don't intend to run your life, but we have to have certain restrictions in our home. I have to decide what is best for you until you are old enough to choose wisely. So that door will remain locked and the subject is closed."

Mark did not want to remember the other harsh words. Of course, David spoke them in anger and he would regret them later. But the session had upset Mark more than he cared to admit, even to himself.

So, when sleep finally came, it had been one of those deep sleeps when the body glides further and further away from reality until it reaches a state of unconsciousness beyond human understanding.

Mark dreamed that he was at the slum apartments late on a summer day. As he looked at the sullen gray structures, they seemed to change before his very eyes, as though someone had touched them with a magic wand. The dirty, unkempt buildings with their falling plaster became clean and white with sparkling windows, shaded by colorful awnings. There were even window boxes in which large red geraniums bloomed in happy profusion. Then Mark noticed he was standing on a broad new sidewalk with a wide belt of green grass and trees. He couldn't help thinking how well kept the lawn was and how healthy the grass looked.

He heard happy children's voices from the rear of the building, and when he walked around to investigate he found a new playground equipped with swings, jungle gyms, a shuffleboard court, and horseshoes for pitching. There was a tennis court and a big ballfield where the boys were busy playing baseball. A distance from the ballfield was a large sparkling blue swimming pool and a smaller wading pool for tiny tots. Everything was perfect. There was even a flower garden in bloom. The apartments seemed to have everything to make the people happy, and when he saw the tenants going about their business, they all looked content. . . . Then a dark cloud covered the sun. When the cloud had passed, the beauty too had disappeared and the dirt, gloom, and squalor had returned. Now everything looked grimmer than before. Mark shuddered and awoke.

What he had seen could be what was supposed to be. It could even be the answer!

Mr. Johnson arrived at the appointed time, and Mark greeted him with a broad smile.

68

"I'm glad to see you, Mr. Johnson. I'm quite excited about my news."

Mr. Johnson took the chair Mark offered him. "I hope it's the news I'm looking for," he said sourly.

"No, it's not at all what we talked about, I'm sorry to say. Mr. Rollins is a stubborn man and he hasn't changed yet. But I've found a way to go around him— a way that I think will enhance our town."

"Tell me about it."

"Since Mr. Rollins refuses to agree to having the apartments torn down, I think that we should fix them up instead. We could make them beautiful, and it would change the whole atmosphere of the north end. Would the town help with certain things, like sidewalks and trees, if we took care of painting and cleaning up?"

Mr. Johnson looked thoughtful.

"I've no authority to say specifically what the town would do, but I'm pretty sure that if you could make the neighborhood a desirable place to live, the town would do its part."

"Do you approve of the idea?"

"Yes, wholeheartedly! The buildings down there are solid. It's the dirt and squalor that we object to. But if you can improve the living conditions, there'd be nothing for us to complain about."

"That's what I'm aiming for, to restore the beauty and dignity of the north end."

"Can you do this without Mr. Rollins' consent?"

"Yes, if we move slowly, repairing things little by little, raising private funds, and giving the people who

69

live there a chance to work at it, too. It will take time though; I'll need at least two years."

"I don't care how long it takes as long as you do begin and show some progress." Mr. Johnson still looked thoughtful. "This puts a new light on the church's usefulness."

Mark smiled. "That's what the church is all about," he said. "Do you know how the first church started? Its very beginning?"

Mr. Johnson shook his head. "I'm afraid I don't, Mr. Cartling. As I told you before, I'm not a church-going man."

"May I tell you about it?"

"Why not? I have a little extra time this morning."

"Well, you perhaps already know, Mr. Johnson, much of what I'm going to say but I will start from the beginning as Christianity really started when Christ was crucified a couple of thousand years ago. The twelve disciples, who had been his closest companions, were frightened and had scattered. The wonderful, solid, new kingdom with their Master as King, about which they had been dreaming, was lost. Their leader, having experienced a cruel death on a shameful cross, was dead and buried. In their sorrow they had forgotten that Christ had foretold all this and that he had also said death would not be able to contain him, that he would rise from the dead. And He did rise! 'Christ is risen!' became the key phrase of Christianity, a phenomenon that changed the whole world. That was the jubilant note of Christianity. Christ appeared to his broken-

70

hearted, stricken followers and told them of a new power that would be given to them—the power to overcome fear and hate, as they went forth into the world to proclaim a new story—that God loved all men and wanted them to have peace, joy, and happiness.

"After they had received that power, the disciples became giants in faith and boldness. They organized the Christian Church to bring together those who had become new persons in this new faith. With a bold love which overcame prison, torture, and death, they spread the Good News all over the world, overcoming evil with good, wrong with right, darkness with light. Soon this new church spread throughout the civilized world, with its strange power changing the lives of men. And the Church grew in wisdom and power, and even after thousands of years, it sent out its missionaries to foreign lands to set men free from their bonds of sin. Wherever the Church was strong, a generation that knew God grew up to help the whole world."

Mark stopped. He had not intended to deliver a sermon, but Mr. Johnson seemed to be such an intent listener that Mark had just kept on.

Then Mr. Johnson spoke. "And where, may I ask, is that Church today, Mr. Cartling?"

Mark's eyes clouded a little and his voice was pained as he answered, "Something has happened to it, Mr. Johnson. You see, it became so easy to become a church member that people lost their vision. And it says in the Bible, that 'where there is no vision, the people will perish.' The Church of today is so busy building more beautiful churches, finding more progressive ways to educate their young, expanding their congregations, that they have forgotten to instruct their people in the origin of the Church's power. They have forgotten Christ's command to go and proclaim the gospel that would change the world from evil to good. I don't blame you for criticizing the Church, Mr. Johnson. But you see only the 'outer garment.' Believe me, the Church still exists, that same Church with its boldness and devotion and passion for spreading the Good News to all people. If I didn't believe that, I couldn't be a minister."

Mr. Johnson stood up, grasping Mark's hand in a firm handshake.

"I like you, Mark Cartling," he said. "Someday you may even see me sitting in your church on a Sunday morning. I believe you have something vital to give to mankind. You are so forthright and honest. I'd better go now. If I stayed much longer, you might even convert me right here on the spot. Imagine that from a hardened old sinner like me."

"As soon as I have some news of progress being made, Mr. Johnson, I'll contact you again. Thank you for your kind words, and believe me, nothing would make me happier than to see you sitting in my church."

The door closed behind Mr. Johnson, and Mark felt a sense of great relief. It had worked out better than he had imagined. God had been good to him. He bowed his head in a silent prayer of thanksgiving. God was on his side, though this was only the beginning. His plan included more than just cleaning up the apartments and beautifying the property. His heart's sincere desire was to reach those hopeless people down there—to get them interested in a church, to find new friends for them, friends who cared what happened to them and could offer them Christian companionship. He would contact Father Smith from the Church of the Sacred Heart, and between them they would sort out the people. Together they would minister to their needs, bringing them good news and hope for a future. The work had to begin slowly so that Mr. Rollins would find no cause to put his foot down or hamper it.

Mark dialed the banker's number.

"Good morning, Mr. Rollins," he said cheerfully. "I'm calling to report on my meeting with Mr. Johnson this morning."

"Oh, yes," said Mr. Rollins. "I'd forgotten all about it. I didn't realize the time was up."

"Well, he was here exactly on time. That man certainly is punctual. But we had a good talk. I had to tell him something. Since I couldn't tell him we were willing to give up the apartments, I told him we would clean things up down there and I asked if the town would do its part by putting in a sidewalk and planting some trees."

"Good for you! Did you get away with that?"

"Yes, Mr. Johnson thought it was a fine idea. He even said he might attend our church sometime."

"That will be the day! ... Well, I suppose we do have to do something down there, but I'm telling you that whatever we do for those people will only be ruined again. You must have some idea as to how you will go about it, so I'll leave that to you. Just spend as little money as possible."

Mark felt sick inside after talking to Mr. Rollins. There was a man who had no vision of God's Church. If Mr. Rollins only knew the elaborate plans Mark had for those apartments! But one day he would see. Having told Mr. Rollins what was happening, Mark felt free to get started.

There were three buildings down there—each with three floors and each floor with six apartments. Every tenement was occupied. Mark didn't know just how many people were involved, but he was anxious to find out.

⪦ 8

WHEN ELSA and Mark were newlyweds, Saturday night had been very special for them; in fact, Elsa had referred to it as "our night." But that was before Mark moved to this big church in Robendale-by-the-Sea where he was so busy that no night could ever be called their own again. But on this particular fall Saturday night, there were no meetings or obligations and the youngsters each had their own plans. Susan had been invited to have dinner with Gary's family and would spend the evening with them. David was taking Eric with him to see a movie on outer space, bribing him with the prospect of a triple-decker hamburger after the show. They all had left early and the parsonage was empty and peaceful.

It's almost too still, thought Elsa, as she picked the last of the deep red chrysanthemums in the garden, almost caressing them as she carried them into the house.

"You beautiful, beautiful flowers," she said. "There'll be no more of you now until next fall, and that is a long time off."

Mark drove in the driveway and found Elsa waiting on the back step for him. He gave her a light kiss.

"How about going out to dinner with me tonight?" he asked.

"No thanks, Mark. I have other plans for us."

"My, my! Is my wife planning to take me out?"

"No such thing, my dear husband. Your wife is planning to have an 'our night' right here in the parsonage. Do you remember how Saturday nights used to be? Our other churches seemed to be so considerate, realizing that a minister needed a night with his family. They never seemed to plan anything to bother you on Saturday nights. Remember how I would fuss a little and after the children were in bed we would have our dinner alone in front of the fire. And do you remember our favorite meal? Waffles with that pure maple syrup and sausages! Well, tonight we are having just that in front of the fire and nothing in any restaurant could taste any better."

"That's wonderful, Elsa! You are a wife after my own heart. Nothing can take the place of the two of us reliving old times. I'll get the logs and get the fire started."

It was a special night for both of them. Elsa had almost forgotten how much fun it was to be just the two of them at a small table with candlelight and a fire in the open hearth. Mark dressed in a pair of slacks and a blue flannel shirt and his comfortable slippers, and

76

Elsa wore a pink hostess gown. This was the way they used to relax, and it had been such a long time since they had been able to feel free to be themselves.

Elsa knew that Mark was pleased and happy as they sat on the sofa watching the tongues of fire leap up and down scattering warmth over the room.

For a while they sat silently, each thinking back on former times in the ministry when the task had not been so hard and the workload so much lighter and their lives simpler and easier. Then Mark broke the silence.

"Would you like to discuss something unpleasant, Elsa?" he asked out of the blue.

Elsa looked up a bit alarmed.

"How could anything be unpleasant on a night like this? I can't think of anything."

"But there is something, honey. And I would like to discuss it with you. For a long time I have kept it to myself, but the burden has been especially heavy because I could not share it with you. I still don't know if it's right to shatter your beautiful world by telling you that you're living in a fool's paradise, that this very ground on which our parsonage stands could open up and swallow us up. Elsa, my world is unsure and shaky. It is hard for me even to admit this; it looks so perfect on the outside."

Elsa felt bewildered. She could feel her heart pounding. Mark was serious. Something was wrong with life.

"I can't imagine what you are talking about, dear," she said, trying to calm her voice. "What are you trying to tell me, Mark?"

77

Mark leaned back heavily.

"It's a long story, Elsa, and an ugly one. I will tell it to you, but you must try to be realistic about it. I will try to draw the curtain aside slowly so you can see my world as it now presents itself. But I need you, my dear. I need you more than I ever needed you before. I need your love and your wisdom and your understanding and co-operation. I am almost desperate. You see, I had wanted to shield you from the blow I received, but tonight I know I can't go on without you. You must stand by my side, and at times, I might even have to lean on you because the future looks dark and uncertain."

Elsa just stared at her husband, unable to grasp the meaning of his strange words. Her throat felt tight and dry but she forced herself to take command of all her composure. If Mark needed her, she must not fail him. Her voice was firm when she spoke.

"Mark," she said, "if you have things to unburden, I will certainly listen. Haven't we always shared the good and the bad together? Don't hold anything back from me. I promise I can take it. I want to know it all. Mark, what have you done?"

Mark laughed in spite of the seriousness of the situation.

"Thank God, Elsa, I haven't done anything. It isn't me! I don't have any confession to make although it might have been simpler if it were me. Elsa, it's the church I have to tell you about, our beautiful church on the hill which we both love so much. It is sick. It has a cancer destroying it. It is self-centered, greedy, and corrupt at its foundation. I have taken up arms against it. There are slum apartments in the North End that our church owns."

As the fire slowly died, Mark began to tell his wife of that day when Mr. Johnson first called on him revealing the story of the apartments, including Mr. Rollins' part in things and the condition of the slum and its people living on Linden Street paying their rent to the church without ever getting repairs done or enough heat or help in their distress. He told of his visits down there and the agony and pain he had felt. Then he told Elsa of the dream that had come to him and the progress that was finally being made. He told Elsa how Bill Lowell, his assistant, had also plunged into the work and what a great help he was, especially now when he was planning to organize the young people to paint and renovate. Now that the money was coming in, some of the apartments were getting new stoves, and Mark was trying to make sure that the heat was plentiful.

Mark talked on and on. The children came home and went to bed. The fire, now just ashes, gave off an eery glow; then it was gone, leaving the fireplace dead and still. But Mark and Elsa still sat on the sofa—Mark talking and Elsa listening.

Elsa's eyes were wide and sorrowful when Mark finished his story.

"I just can't believe it, Mark! How could a thing like that take place in a church and how could a man like Mr. Rollins who seems so sweet and charming most of the time be so hard and unfeeling. Our church has plenty of money to meet its budget. This whole situation seems so unnecessary to me. I can't even associate it with the life of a church."

"Elsa, it could not happen in all churches. But, you see, a community church has more freedom in its methods of bringing in income. The finance committee is made up mainly of business men and they run that function of the church. I know many such men who are soft-hearted and charming and even charitable in their public life, but who are hard, stubborn, and unyielding when it comes to business. Mr. Rollins is one of those. To him, this function of the church is just business and that's the way he treats it."

"But it isn't right!"

"Elsa, it could have started out right. I think when Mr. Rollins first invested in that inexpensive property, he felt he could make a profit and provide a service at the same time. The rent is very low. Where else can people rent a three-room apartment with heat for fifty dollars a month in these times? Apparently he felt that poor people should be given some kind of a roof over their heads, and that was right thinking. But the wrong lies in the things he has robbed those people of, such as dignity. His own feeling is that they are not used to a better environment than what they create for themselves. If they create a pigpen, then they can live in it. He feels it would be a waste of money to improve things that would never be taken care of. But that is judging people before they are given a chance. There are many

80

wonderful people down there who long for beauty and a chance to dream dreams that might come true. When things get so bad down on Linden Street that the town had to step in, then I felt that as a minister I had to get involved also."

"And now they shall have a chance, Mark. We will give it to them. I can't wait to get started. I want to go down there to see what I can do, and I know Carol will help me. Oh, just wait! Carol and I will be the interior decorators and help them fix things. And here is a thought, Mark. Couldn't we share our old furniture with them? We don't need it now and if we move, we could use some new things."

"Is that so, Mrs. Cartling," Mark joked. "Don't forget, I might be out on my ear the day Mr. Rollins finds out what I am doing. But I am certainly willing to share what we have. First we must find out what is most needed in furnishings and I will leave that to you. Do with the furniture as you wish, but part of my heart is still in some of those old pieces when I remember how we had to struggle to buy them."

Elsa smiled.

"Our struggle seems so long ago now. I am afraid all this abundance might have spoiled me a bit."

The next day after their Sunday dinner, Elsa and Mark drove down to Linden Street. For a while they sat in the car looking at life as it went on there on a Sunday afternoon. The whole street looked sadly gloomy although music drifted out of an open window and some boys were playing ball on an empty lot. The litter that had been everywhere when Mark first took on the job was gone and there were plenty of trash cans with covers and new garbage cans in back of the buildings. The exterior could have looked a lot worse. But it was when Mark took Elsa into the homes that Elsa's heart cried. The rooms were in terrible condition with torn paper, plasterless ceilings, exposed pipes, gaping holes and dark, dirty kitchens. She was constantly aware of the children's eyes following her wherever she went. She smiled at them, but they did not return her smile. They were not happy, and some even looked hungry. Mark and Elsa did not stay long, and on the way home they spoke very little. When finally they drove into the parsonage driveway, Elsa wiped a tear from her eye.

Mark looked at her tenderly.

"It did throw you, Elsa, didn't it? It isn't a pretty place to see."

"It wasn't just seeing the property, Mark. I knew it would not be a pretty sight. But the gloomy atmosphere got me, the depression. That little black boy with those enormous brown eyes with such sadness in them was such a good looking boy. He couldn't have been more than six, but there seemed to be no gladness in him. I think the picture of his face will gnaw at me until I can get him to smile. One day I hope he will let me hug him."

"That's *you*, Elsa! And that is why we all need you. I can get the workers to repair the material things, but what those people need more than anything else is someone to love them and care about the little things in their lives. You will take care of that!"

For a while, Elsa found it hard to sleep at night. Her warm generous heart suffered and if she fell asleep, she would awaken suddenly wondering how things were in the North End. Was a child sobbing because he was hungry or lonely or afraid of the dark? So many of the mothers and fathers were forced to leave their children alone while they went out to work at odd jobs, here and there, even at night. Others might visit friends, trying to forget the terrible conditions surrounding them. But what about the babies? Did they lay there crying for their bottles or to be changed? Perhaps their little bottoms were raw from neglect and they cried because they hurt. Elsa was in agony. Was there enough milk for the children? She had seen an old man with deeply hollowed cheeks sitting in a wheelchair. He had just looked at her with a resignation in his eyes she would never forget. How could she have so much when all those people had so little? Those people lived in the shadows in the slums; they just existed. Perhaps they had never known what it was to be happy and carefree or even filled with good food.

More and more of Elsa's time was spent doing little things for her newly adopted friends. She no longer had time for her leisurely walks, her reading, or even her fancy baking for her family. She hardly ever arrived at the apartments without something she had made especially for the children—big gingerbread mamas or papas or brownies or cupcakes. She took turns distributing them and it gave her such pleasure. Her life took on a new meaning. The children smiled now when she came with her basket; they danced around her longing for her to share the contents of her basket. Never had Elsa felt more rewarded, but she knew that until the apartments were repaired and their homes were in order with the children well-dressed and smiling, she would not stop giving of her time. It was wonderful to work with Mark, to hear him laugh and joke as he did in the old days. She knew that Mark too had to serve to be happy.

The Lowells worked hard, too, and the two pastors had formed a team to wipe out sin, corruption, poverty, and filth. Their friendship grew, too, and Elsa felt that God himself must be smiling down on them from His heaven because they were doing His work here on earth.

Elsa and Mark were both surprised and happy when many people outside the church became interested in helping with the project, taking on special tasks such as finding stoves and refrigerators in working order or repairable televisions. Everything was fixed and then put to use for the poor.

In the midst of their work Elsa suddenly realized that the Church, God's Church, was not a building; it was people . . . people who came from all directions with love in their hearts, people who were willing to step out into the darkness of the world with a candle to spread the light and bring the good news that God loved all mankind and wanted them to come home to

His kingdom to be made whole. These people did not just feed the body, but the soul also—that restless, yearning part of man that never found peace until it rested in its Creator. Yes, Elsa could see all these workers in her mind's eye. She could see hands reaching out —gentle, kind hands—willing to give and to touch; warm, sturdy hands—ready to lift and to caress, to bless and to pray. These were the symbols of the real Church, the Church that not even the fires of hell could destroy.

"Mark," said Elsa one night when the wind was whistling outside the parsonage and she and Mark were seated discussing the next step of their project. "Mark, I know our dream will become reality one day. I have won the confidence of many of my new friends. They know my friendship is real. You know, they aren't looking for charity; they are looking for help to become the wonderful people they were meant to be in the first place."

"You are right," said Mark, "and the best thing that ever happened to them was when I came to my senses and took you into my confidence. Elsa, God bless you! You are one in a million!"

And those words rang in Elsa's mind and heart, crowning the whole project. Mark's love and confidence was really all she ever wanted.

~ 9

On a beautiful, crisp fall afternoon, Mark stepped out of his study and stood for a moment, struck by the view that unfolded before his eyes. He could see the ocean clearly through the trees, some of which had already shed their leaves, making room for the blue ocean to peek through. Very few churches could boast of a view changing with each season to one even more breathtaking than the one before.

Now in the late afternoon the sun sinking in the west scattered its gold so lavishly on the hillside that Mark felt as if a heavenly benediction blessed the very spot on which he stood. Then he spotted Father Smith coming slowly up the steep hill. Mark stood waiting.

"Am I having a caller?" Mark asked. "Or are you just out for a stroll?"

Father Smith flashed a broad smile. "I was going to pay you a call, but the day is so beautiful I'd be just as happy to walk and talk."

"Fine! Let's go down through the park."

Together they started down the hill; the air had a tang of burning leaves; trees stood flaming in rainbow colors, each flaunting its various shades of red and gold. With the late afternoon sun pouring down, the park looked like a fairyland.

For a while the two men walked in silence. They met here often. Mark valued Father Smith's friendship, his dry humor and quick wit.

Finally Mark said, "Well, which is it this time? Am I losing a sheep, or is one of yours straying my way?"

This was how they usually teased each other as they discussed inevitable changes in membership as a result of young people falling in love.

Father Smith's face clouded for a minute, and his voice was serious when he replied.

"I wish I could laugh about this one, Mark, but I'm finding myself in an uncomfortable situation. Your daughter Susan has come to me requesting instruction in Gary's faith. She says she has made no decision, but she does want to study our church before she makes her choice."

Mark slackened his pace. Father Smith's words had taken him by surprise.

"Father John," he said, using his friend's intimate title, "Elsa and I are aware of the situation. One of them will have to change if they do marry. But they're still so young that I hope they'll wait awhile. To be honest with you, in my heart I had hoped that Gary would come over to Susan's faith."

"Their age is the reason I wanted to consult you, Mark. If Susan were an adult, I couldn't have divulged any of this. We Catholics don't steal sheep, I want you to know. We just woo them over to our side. But Susan is still a little lamb. I'm sure in her heart she is quite confused and it might be some time before she understands the great mystery of believing."

"Yes, she is a lamb, a very precious one to her parents, but she is very persistent. I'm sorry that our Church leaves her cold. She has many doubts about God."

"Are you against my instructing her?"

"No, but even if I were, I couldn't be. Susan must have the freedom to choose her own course in life. I'm glad she's interested enough to find out what Gary has been taught since his youth. He's an exceptionally fine boy with high Christian principles. We couldn't ask for a finer young man for our girl."

"Nothing may come of this, but as a priest before God, I shall do my best to convince her. Now, with your permission, I can do it with a light heart."

"You go ahead," said Mark. "If Susan is persuaded to change her faith, it must be her own choice."

But even as Mark was saying the words, he knew that he must find a chance to talk to Susan, too. Perhaps he could relate to her some things he had neglected in the past.

"I'm glad we talked this over, Mark. It's amazing to think how much we've mellowed since your arrival. Now we can be brothers even though we carry different labels."

88

Mark shook Father Smith's hand. "Thank you for coming to me and thank you for being my friend. I'm convinced that the true Church isn't contained in a building and that denominations don't matter before God. He judges us by the faith in our hearts and what we do for mankind. . . ."

"Well, some people are predicting that the institution of the Church is doomed, but I disagree with them. I believe that the true Church of God will move forward in majestic union. It shall not be moved from its foundation laid two thousand years ago. Christ lives and His Church shall live!"

They were back at the hill by the parsonage.

"How about having dinner with us?" asked Mark.

"Thank you, Mark, but my housekeeper has my meal all prepared. I'll take you up on it some other time."

They parted and Mark climbed the hill toward the church. He was deep in thought. The news concerning Susan bothered him. Hadn't he been a good father who had tried to be understanding? Was he losing Susan the way he was losing David? It must not happen. There must be a way for them to communicate again.

He sat down on the broad church steps, his favorite place. The sinking sun had turned the ocean into a sea of gold.

What was it with this new generation? Would they be up to taking over the future? They had such fabulous dreams, these youngsters of tomorrow, as they set out to conquer outer space. Yes, they would build bigger and better spaceships, and brave men would dare to step into the unknown, beckoning their generation to follow. What was in store for them in worlds filled with wonder and danger? If only they would explore the spiritual world as eagerly and diligently. There was a great need for brave young people willing to explore the Kingdom of God and to beckon others to follow. The greatest task of a minister of God was to plant the necessary seeds in the minds of the new generation. A new world was waiting—free from war and sorrow and disappoinment—if someone could just convince them to take up the prophet's mantle and help it come to pass.

Mark's reverie was broken by the sound of running feet, as Eric came up the hill, waving and calling out to him.

"You must come quickly, Dad. There's trouble on Linden Street. A Sandra Jones called. She needs you and Mom called the study, but you weren't there."

Mark met his son.

"I was walking with Father Smith, Eric. Run home and tell your mother that I'm on my way."

Linden Street was where the apartments were located, although no one ever referred to the section as anything but "the apartments." Perhaps when the beautification project was completed, the street would be called by its right name again. Mark hoped so; he liked the name.

As he drove toward the north end, he wondered what had happened in the Jones' household? Was someone ill or in trouble? The Joneses' apartment had been the first to be renovated and never had there been more grateful tenants. They seemed to be a nice couple with one child, Sandra, who was twelve or thirteen, a bright, dark-haired girl with sparkling brown eyes.

Mark found Sandra sitting on the apartment step when he parked his car in front of the building. Her eyes were not sparkling now as she ran to meet him.

"Thank you for coming, Pastor Cartling," she called out. "I didn't know what to do or whom to call. Dad was very drunk and so abusive to Mom. They had an awful fight. I don't know what has happened up there since because I stayed out here after I called you. But I'm scared."

Tears began to roll down her cheeks and she tried hard to brush them away.

Mark put his arm around her. "You did the right thing to call me, Sandra. Remember I'm your friend and you can always call on me. Now, let's go up and see. Perhaps everything has calmed down."

Hurriedly they mounted the dark stairs to the second floor. Everything seemed quiet on the outside. Sandra knocked and then opened the apartment door slowly. Mrs. Jones was seated at the kitchen table with her head in her hands. She looked up as the door opened, her eyes red from crying. She did not know that her daughter had phoned Mark and she assumed this was just a routine visit.

"Come in," she said softly. "This is a bad time for you to call. I'm not feeling very well and Larry is not at his best either. Sandra, go to your room. I'd like to talk to Mr. Cartling."

Sandra disappeared into her bedroom, and Mark seated himself beside Mrs. Jones at the table.

"Can I help you?" he asked.

"I think I'm beyond help. My marriage seems to be on the rocks. Right now my husband is sleeping off his last bottle of whiskey. I can't stop him from drinking and he doesn't know when to stop."

"Perhaps when he's sober, I can talk to him."

"I don't think it would help. Nothing helps any more. I was so sure with our apartment fixed up and everything around us so nice that he would try to stop. But no, not Larry. He's sick, I'm afraid, but even so, he makes our home a hell."

"Why don't you and Sandra come home with me for a few hours? You need to get away for a spell. I'm sure Elsa has enough dinner for two more. And when you come back, things might not seem so grim."

Mark finally persuaded Mrs. Jones to come along and an hour later they were all seated around the table in the parsonage where there was more than enough for them all.

After dinner they had a long talk, both Elsa and Mark trying to counsel with Mrs. Jones while Sandra was off with Susan.

Never had Mark heard more despair in a woman's voice. She could see no solution, no light for the future, and nothing to build on. To think that Mrs. Jones was just one of the thousands of women who faced the same problem, who fought bravely, and finally gave up because their strength wore out, made Mark depressed.

"Larry is such a fine person in himself," Mrs. Jones confided. "He is smart, but he loses one job after another. Today he was fired again. I can't blame his employers; he drinks on the job. Poor Larry is a slave to drinking—and he can't break away by himself."

"We must do something to help him, Mrs. Jones. If he has the fine qualities you say he has, I'll talk to him. I can give him a job working on the apartments for the time being. If he needs a friend, I'll be there. Perhaps I can introduce him to someone who has had the same problem and licked it. And remember, for God nothing is impossible."

"I wish I could believe that. Long ago I did have a faith that lifted me above the dark clouds and made me very happy. But it isn't there any more."

"But it will return," Elsa assured her. "And if you want a friend, I'd like to be yours. Just don't give up. You have a dear, sweet daughter who needs you more than ever."

"I wish you would come to our church," said Mark. "I'm sure you'd make many friends there and it would give you some new interests."

"I'm afraid I have very little time. I work in the school cafeteria. It's good work and I am home when Sandra gets there. But there's very little extra time for other things. We haven't been in a church in years."

"Perhaps you'll try to come on Sunday mornings. There's a bus that goes directly from your home up to the hill."

They talked for a long while. By the time Mark drove

the Joneses home, he had quite an insight into their lives. Now he realized even more clearly that the Church had to find the lost and bewildered to give them hope and confidence in the future. Both Mrs. Jones' and Sandra's spirits seemed to have risen and Mark had a feeling that for them this was a start in the right direction.

After Sandra and her mother had returned to their apartment, Mark sat for a while looking at the cold buildings. He could almost sense the hostility there, the discontent and misery that even the darkness could not hide. He knew he had to reach these people, to help them, and to minister to them. Perhaps this was his real mission in Robendale-by-the-Sea.

The Joneses were just one family in need of help. But there were so many, many more living here. He must help them all.

Mark heard a baby cry and a tired, curt voice telling it to shut up. People went in and came out of the buildings like shadows slowly passing by. Then, realizing the lateness of the hour, Mark started home. Elsa was waiting for him with a hug and a cup of hot coffee.

"I'm so glad you brought Nellie Jones and her daughter here, Mark," she said. "I do want to help them; they have such a cross to bear. Our family has so much—our love for each other, the children, this beautiful home, and God's great love. How can we make amends to all those people who have to struggle so hard? My heart breaks when I think of that family. How can Nellie keep going? And that poor, little girl! She shouldn't have

94

such heavy burdens to carry. I wonder if Mr. Jones was awake when they got home. You must go down there tomorrow and talk to that man, Mark. How wonderful it would be if we could bring them all some happiness."

Mark drew his wife closer.

"You know, Elsa," he said tenderly. "It's strange that in all the years of my ministry I've never really seen God's work as clearly as now. It's as if hands are reaching out everywhere . . . as if voices are calling day and night, 'Come here and help us! Show us God! Give us light! We are lost and bewildered.'"

They stood quietly for a moment, holding each other close, each breathing a prayer for power to do God's will.

The same thoughts stayed with Mark for days afterward until they had imbedded themselves into his soul. Never had the ministry been more important; never had there been a greater challenge; never had the field been more ready for harvest; and never had the workers been so few. Now he felt a conviction as never before and he was burning to get started. The apartments were just the beginning. They were his test and he must not fail. How grateful he was that he had been aroused from his former lethargy. He would be true to his calling as he ventured out into the dark world, carrying a light that no evil wind could extinguish.

He had almost forgotten about Susan. Her predicament had seemed so important that day Father Smith had called. But lately there had been many things on Mark's mind that had pushed her to the back of his thoughts. He had meant to talk to her. She must be fairly serious, since Father Smith had felt it necessary to come to Mark to discuss the matter. It was a very gracious gesture on the priest's part, and perhaps, Mark thought, he even hoped that Susan would not stray from her own faith because it would hurt Mark and Elsa so deeply. Father Smith was a kind and wise man.

One afternoon when Mark arrived home, he found Susan alone in the family room and seized the opportunity to talk with her.

"Can you give me a few minutes, Susan?" he asked, sitting down beside her on the davenport.

Susan dropped the magazine she was reading and smiled at Mark.

"Sure, Dad. We don't have many chances to talk any more."

"I want you to know that Father Smith came to see me a while ago and he told me about your taking instruction from him."

Susan looked surprised. "I didn't think a priest would do that. After all, my going to him was in confidence."

"I think Father Smith felt it a kindness. Your mother and I are not very happy about it, dear. You're still a little girl and we love you."

"Maybe it's just as well you know. But I'm not a little girl and it's not like I'm joining the Catholic Church. I just want to know what they have to offer. Gary seems to get a lot out of it."

"Aren't you happy in your own faith, honey?"

"No, sometimes my religion leaves me cold. There's

96

so little to it! I'm not always sure I can believe things just because the Church says they're so. Sometimes I'm not even sure there's a God. If there is, why does He permit evil? Why does He permit so much suffering and war and hate? If God is what you preach, why doesn't He do something to show us his power?"

"Honey, we must not question God! God did not create evil or suffering or war or hate. Man did that himself. If God stepped in and did something about every situation, then we would be no more than puppets. But if, of our own free will, we lived according to God's laws, none of these horrible things would exist. But living that way takes faith. We don't have faith in our minds; it is born in our souls, and it either grows stronger or it fades away. Faith is like a seed that has been planted. If it doesn't get water and sunshine and care, it dies. When God touches us with His own spirit, we first become alive and then we really understand. But to find this faith, a person must first surrender himself to God."

"You've told me all that before, but it doesn't work for me. Maybe someday I'll find it, but I'll have to find it in my own way. Don't worry about me. Gary and I will find some way that will work for both of us. . . . Now may I go back to my story?"

"Sure! I guess I can take a hint. We must have talked enough. Thank you for the time you allowed out of your busy life."

Susan picked up her magazine and left the room.

Well, that was that!

And then there was David. Suddenly Mark knew that he had been wrong. He had sinned against the boy! All that ambition David had had to build a ship to go to Mars—how he must have dreamed about it and counted and figured, trying to fit things together in that small basement room. He had made one mistake and everything was lost. Mark remembered how unhappy the boy had been, as if he had lost life itself. He had suffered the burns, the cuts, and the loss of all he had worked for, and what had his father done? He had scolded him severely and locked the door to his laboratory, telling him he could never use it again. David had pleaded with him, but Mark had been firm and the door had remained locked even though Mark noticed how David had changed. He became stubborn. His marks at school dropped way down. And he seemed to hate the world. How blind Mark had been as a father. He should have forgiven him, offering him understanding and the courage to start again. Well, he would! He would tell David he was sorry and admit that he had been unwise. He would unlock that lab door and give David the money to start over.

Thinking about it, his heart was light. The change had come as he ministered to those people in the dark apartment block. That was what was important in life—to plant good seed and give love. God's love to a lost world.

✌ 10

TIME MOVED SWIFTLY. It was the busiest year that Mark could ever remember and the winter was almost passed before he finally got around to trying to set things straight with David. But one morning he suddenly decided that this was the time. David had been very sullen of late and the strain between father and son was almost at the breaking point. Now Mark was really willing to humble himself, admit to David that he had been wrong and ask his forgiveness. In fact this very morning he would go to David's room and have a good talk with him; they would come to an understanding and it would be like old times. He and David would go down to breakfast together. Just the thought of this decision lifted Mark's spirit and he found himself singing in the shower, the way he used to do when life had seemed easy, before his church had began to fail him, laying a heavy burden on his heart and mind. Yes, this morning was beautiful! Outside the sun was shining from a clear blue sky. There was something about a clear morning that made Mark feel it was good to be alive, and today there was a coziness about the parsonage that warmed his heart and made him especially grateful for his home and family.

Sometimes, he thought to himself, a minister is so busy taking care of other people that he neglects his own family. Well, he would try to rectify that mistake today, and never again would he fail his own children.

Suddenly Mark realized how happily and completely a child could lose himself in his own self-made world. In his own childhood he had had that rock. With David it was his spaceship. Mark realized belatedly what it would have done to him if his dad had forbidden him to go to his rock ever again because he had made a mistake or pulled a stunt of some kind. But that was what he—Mark—had done to his son; he had taken David's dearest treasure away from him and left him lost and bewildered without his workshop. All David had really done, he kept repeating in his own mind, was to have an accident. Poor David! His happy world had been shattered, but instead of consoling the boy, Mark had meted out a severe punishment. Well, now he would make things right again.

Mark walked across the hall to David's room and knocked on the door. "David," he called softly.

David was a sound sleeper, so Mark knocked again, this time harder. Still there was no answer, so he opened the door and stepped in, to stand there, frozen in place.

David was not there. His bed was made up neatly; the room was picked up; the windows were closed. On the bedspread was pinned a large note. Mark snatched it up, staring at his son's large handwriting which he knew so well. He read it once, then twice, then a third time, as if he were trying to grasp its message:

Dear Mom,

I am leaving the parsonage tonight while you all are asleep. I have been planning this ever since the day I found my workshop locked. I knew then that Dad would never understand and that I could never adjust to his strict rules. That is why I am begging you, Mom, *please* hold Dad back from calling the police or trying to find me. I am not going to do anything foolish. I plan to look for a job and when I find it, to work hard and make a new life in my own world. I have to find myself because I have felt lost for such a long time. As soon as I have found myself, I will get in touch with you, Mom, and let you know where I am. Please, please trust me and let me go, for this is the way it must be. Don't worry about me and don't cry. I don't love you less because I'm going, but I can't stop resenting Dad. I know it's not right to drop out of school, but I am old enough, if you'll make it right with the school, and I promise to make it up later.

Thank you for standing by me.

I love you,
Dave

Something seemed to whither and die within Mark. All he could grasp was that he had been too late. Just yesterday David had been here, sitting with the rest of the family around the dinner table. He would never know what his son had been thinking last night nor would he have any idea where David had gone or how long he would be gone.

Downstairs in the dining room, Elsa and Eric were already seated at the table watching the birds outside the large picture window, laughing as two birds began to fight over a piece of suet in the feeder.

As Mark stepped into the archway, he met Elsa's smiling eyes. He wanted to speak, but the words would not come. Instead, he handed her the note, then took his place at the table. A hush fell over the room as Elsa read David's words. Her hands were shaking and when she looked up at her husband, there were tears in her eyes.

"Is he really gone?" she asked, as if Mark's answer would change the written words.

Mark nodded. "He's not in his room and the bed is still made up. He must have gone in the night just as he says."

Elsa struggled to hold back the tears, but the three of them hardly touched their breakfast. Only the looks that passed from one to the other showed how deeply they cared. It would be hard to break the news to Susan when she returned from spending the night with a friend. Though Eric did not fully understand the impact of the news, he was sad as he went off to school, perhaps to share the tragedy with Bernie. After he had gone, Elsa and Mark faced each other.

"We have to find him, Elsa." Mark's words were

almost a sob. "If we have to turn the world upside down, we have to find him."

"I don't think he'll be easy to find, Mark. David is a serious boy and he always calculates and plans before he does anything. He wanted to go and we might just have to accept this."

"But it was I, Elsa, who drove our son away from home."

Elsa put her arm around Mark's shoulder.

"You mustn't blame yourself, dear," she said. "You did what you thought was best for David. Your punishment might have been the immediate cause for his running away, but he's really running away from himself. That's why we must let him go so he can find himself again. My heart aches at not knowing where he is, but if he comes home of his own free will, it may help us all restore our family relationship. Perhaps he'll lose a year in school, but he can always catch up later. And we must pray, Mark, pray for David as never before. You might have made a mistake, but you meant well. I'll have to go to the school to explain David's absence."

"What will you tell them?"

"I'll tell the truth, that he was unhappy because he couldn't work on his invention, so he left home."

"We'll go and tell them together," said Mark.

Dark, lonely days followed. Perhaps in his heart Mark hoped that his son would find the world too much to tackle and would come home soon. A few days after

David's departure, Mark discovered that his son had withdrawn the money from his bank account. There had been only a little over $100.00 which could not last too long when paying for food and lodging. Perhaps when his money ran out, David would come home. But weeks passed with no sign of him.

One night at the dinner table, Eric tried to be helpful.

"You know, if Dave had built his spaceship in another place and had taken off for Mars," he suggested excitedly, "he would have been a great guy and had his picture in all the papers and we would be proud of him."

"Yes, that would have been exciting, Eric," said Mark. "But David didn't have enough money to build a real spaceship, so that couldn't have happened. But we'll be proud of him just the same. Wherever he goes, whatever he does, we'll be proud of him."

It had been awkward explaining David's absence to the young people of the church, and the congregation was sure to wonder when they didn't see him. So Mark had to find a way to let them know. He decided to tell them in his Sunday morning sermon a couple of weeks after David's departure. He set his topic, "Family Relations in Our Modern Times," to serve this purpose and directed a few sentences to David's situation.

"We have had a revolution in our own peaceful household recently," he said, trying to keep his voice light. "One morning we found our older son David missing. He informed us in a note that he had gone looking for work in order to make his own way in the world. He didn't want to alarm us, but only to exercise his rights. Although we are deeply concerned, we're hoping that he will return soon, much wiser and more tolerant of his parents."

That was all!

During the week that followed, the telephone rang often in both parsonage and church study, and Elsa and Mark tried to answer the many questions tactfully. People sympathized and tried to comfort them, admired their courage and resolution as they tried to understand their son's needs. But even as they answered the various questions, both Elsa and Mark hid beneath the surface the sadness and worry they felt.

The Cartlings' second year in the Robendale parish was drawing to a close. It had been an eventful year, filled to the brim with experiences, both happy and sorrowful. Now it was June again!

Susan was graduating from high school with high honors. She had been a delight to her parents and they were pleased that in the fall she was to enter Wellsley. This was a big year for Susan and next year it should be David who would graduate. . . . He would be missing from his class if he didn't return soon. But David was sure to reason that out and be back before it was too late. That was what his father was hoping and praying.

In July the Cartlings would have a month's vacation. Mark was looking forward to that time more than ever. His mind, body, and soul were all weary. It would be good to get up to New Hampshire, to go back to dear old friends and to see the little gray church again. They had rented Mr. Swan's small ski chalet for the month.

Just to breathe in the mountain air, Mark thought, should give him a new lease on life, and when the summer was over, he would have to work harder than ever to make his dreams a reality.

The apartment project, which had been in full swing in the spring, had begun to slow down in the hot summer. There was no hotter place than Linden Street when the sun beat down. And when the odor rose from filled garbage cans and uncollected trash, it was no pleasure to be there. The street was a barren, colorless bit of land with stucco buildings on treeless plots. But next June it would be different, Mark told himself. There were enough people interested in the work now to make Mark feel sure that a miracle could take place.

And as soon as his vacation was over and the family was back in the parsonage, Mark plunged right in. He used every opportunity to get to know the tenants. He even opened discussion groups in the parsonage two nights a week so that people could come to talk things out, and many of them did just that. They emptied out their fears and frustrations, which Mark tried to replace with spiritual food that would heal and comfort.

Father Smith was a great help, too; he filled the need for his own lost sheep and offered them security and shelter under the protection of their church. The Hylands were already settled in the Church of the Sacred Heart. Albert Hyland was now well and strong again and had taken over the burden of providing for his family.

106

Then there was Larry Jones. Mark was pleased with the way he was trying to help himself. Every day he worked hard repairing the apartments, and so far there had been money to pay him each week. On a couple of occasions, temptation had proved too strong and Larry had skipped a few days' work. But each time he returned, he seemed more determined than ever to stay "on the wagon." There were so many more like the Joneses living in the apartments and they needed help and encouragement desperately. Mark sympathized with their problem and had learned to be patient and understanding, knowing that a habit was not licked over night. Misfits, Mr. Rollins had called them. Well, there were plenty of misfits, but Mark never gave up. They were all people with hearts and souls and feelings, lost along the way, and as a minister he had to love them all and try to lead them back to the safe road. But his heart ached for them when he saw them trying. They were young and old, black and white. Some were slaves to drugs or drink, some to laziness, and some were slaves to failure. They needed individual help and advice, but most of all, they needed to feel that within themselves were talents yet to come to the surface.

They all seemed to like Pastor Cartling and many tried to show their appreciation by attending his church on Sunday mornings. It did Mark's heart good to see them among the members of the congregation. They were not too particular about their dress; some came in slacks and blue jeans, without ties or jackets. Mark was so pleased to see them there that he did not stop to consider the reactions of his church members. But he soon learned. His congregation was shocked and horrified. This had never happened before. But when their children began to invite the young people from Linden Street to join their activities, Mark could feel the tension mounting. He was proud of his unbiased young people who accepted their unlearned, rough counterparts with ease. It was only their parents who refused to open their hearts and arms to the poor. Mark wished that the older group would take a cue from their children.

Looking back on the situation a few months later, Mark realized that this was the beginning of his fall from grace. No minister of the Robendale Church had ever encouraged such an invasion before. The poor and the needy had always kept to themselves, too sinful, perhaps, to attend this church. Members of Mark's church had never considered it their Christian duty to love, help, or befriend the unlovely. Mark could feel their coolness on Sunday mornings as he stood at the door to greet them, and he noticed that some members went out the side exit so they would not have to shake his hand.

The telephone calls came during the week. Why not open a mission church for those people in the north end so they wouldn't have to travel so far? some suggested. Some hoped that Mark was not considering giving these people church membership.

As fall approached, the congregation had split into two groups—one willing to work with their senior minister; the other determined to block him.

Mark's first open warning came from Bill Lowell.

"You know," he said, "I feel I must tell you that there's a lot of grumbling among our members. They don't want those people from the north end in the church. They feel that you have encouraged them to invade both the worship services and other activities. The people of the Community Church consider themselves a cultured, dignified, above-average group and they don't want to change. They want the church to stay as it was before you came."

"And what do you think about this, Bill?" asked Mark solemnly.

Bill took his time answering.

"This is my bread and butter, too. It's a great church and I'm paid more here than most assistant ministers. To tell the truth, Mark, I wish you'd let things be. There's plenty for us to do right here. Why start trouble?"

"In other words, Bill, it's all right to clean up the apartments and to smile and be friendly to the tenants. But to ask them to participate with us in the Church of God is out of the question. Their bodies and environment we may care for, but their souls and spiritual life are not our concern."

"Oh, Mark, I'm not quite that callous. Perhaps this isn't the church for those people. There are plenty of churches between Linden Street and our Holy Hill. Perhaps we should direct the people to one of them instead of causing trouble here. For goodness' sake, Mark, let's bear in mind that this is a sophisticated church—cultured and refined. Its members are not overly religious. In fact, there are times when I think that what they really worship is the beauty, name, and history of their church. Do you think they give much thought to God? But if you ask my advice, I'd say let them stay as they are. Don't burst the bubble."

"Bill," said Mark, weighing his words thoughtfully, "as far as my job here is concerned, I am a servant of God and I have definite convictions about what is right and wrong. Who are we to say which people are the best? The members of our congregation are a lucky lot who were born rich and brought up in refined surroundings. But in faith, perhaps they're not so lucky. To God the poor and struggling are worth just as much. I have vowed to proclaim the gospel to rich and poor alike. I might not approve of the way the poor dress to attend church, but dress is not that important. I'd rather have them come as they are than not at all. Just now these people from the north end are the greater part of my ministry."

"I know you're right!" said Bill. "And I do admire your courage, Mark. But several people have asked me to talk to you, so now I have. You have to follow your own conscience, of course, but I'm sorry that you're undermining your position. I trust you know what you're doing."

And Mark did know! Words like Bill's made him even more determined to befriend those people and help them. He felt sad about the rift he had caused and even sadder that his church could not work with him on this important mission. At times it upset Mark that the gap between the church and minister was widening, that they failed to understand each other. But now Mark planned each day cautiously so that nothing in the church would be neglected. Because of the feelings, Mark must see to the apartments on the side. And there was plenty to do each day, more than time allowed for. One thing did puzzle him. That was that Mr. Rollins had never interfered with the work on the apartments. He neither praised nor complained.

When word reached Mark that Mr. and Mrs. Rollins were planning a trip around the world, he was delighted. They would be gone until spring, and that would allow more freedom to complete the apartment projects.

The Rollinses were given a nice send-off. The Board of Directors gave a large party for them, which put Mr. Rollins at his best. When he shook hands with Mark and Elsa, he was all smiles. The size of the party had assured him of his own importance and he felt at peace with the world. The welfare and interests of the people of Linden Street seemed to be left in Mark's hands. Perhaps, Mr. Rollins felt that this project came under the pastoral category, not the financial. Mark hoped that was the case.

After the Rollinses had left the village, Mark plunged even deeper into the work at the north end, spending many odd hours on the project. The work was showing progress, and he wanted it completed by the time he reached his third anniversary at the church. There was not a minute to lose.

~ 11

"No, Susan, nothing shocks me any more," said Elsa, trying to look nonchalant. "Something has happened to our sane world! When David left home, we were upset to find our lovely family in discord. Now it's you, Susan. I would never have dreamt that you would cause us such worry and concern."

Susan was home from college for a long weekend. She and Elsa were alone in the family room where Susan had curled up on the sofa like a kitten. She looked stunning tonight in her black velvet pants suit trimmed with gold braid, her blond hair falling over her shoulders. Susan's eighteen-year-old carefreeness annoyed Elsa tonight. How could she sit there smiling as though nothing had happened when she just upset Elsa's whole world?

Susan looked at her mother wide-eyed. "Is it such a crime to drop out of college? You act as if I were doing something dreadful."

"Yes, it is a crime and it is dreadful and more than that for a girl who made the high-school honor roll for three years and won a scholarship and all sorts of awards, who has been accepted at a college of such high standing—the envy of all those girls who failed— just to toss it all away like some worthless thing. I'm deeply disappointed in you, Susan."

"Well, I'm not dropping out to do nothing. I've chosen a career. I know what I want. Colleges aren't so hot any more. There's a lot of discord and trouble and more weird things going on than you're aware of. I've loved nursing ever since I worked in the hospital last summer as an aid. I'll be proud to train as a nurse, and when I'm ready, I'll marry Gary. I will never be out of a job and I'll be doing something useful. I don't see that it's anything so awful."

"Your dad will be heartbroken. He's already carrying a heavy load of sorrow and worry over David. You know how much education means to him. I just wonder what Eric will think up in a few years to torment his parents. There will be something, you can be sure of that."

"I don't see what Dad has to do with my life. Why should he object? I know what I want, and I'll do very well. You just wait and see!"

Elsa sighed a deep sigh. "I wish you were little again! I wish you all were small so I could be close to you. All of you are going your own way and we're drifting apart. We don't even know how to communicate any more."

Elsa blinked back the tears. It wasn't like her to talk

this way. As a rule, she was happy and understanding, but the thought of Susan dropping out of college seemed to be more than she could bear.

Susan pushed her hair back from her forehead, and gave her mother a warm, almost forgiving, smile.

"Mom," she said, "you're right. We are far, far apart in our thinking. You still live in the old world—the secure, good, solid world where right was right and wrong was wrong. Happiness came to you if you lived a virtuous, good life. God sent angels to protect you from harm and sin. You fell in love, married, and had children whom you molded in your own pattern. You were proud of fitting them with cloaks that you had worn and you wanted them to walk in your shoes. But that world doesn't exist any more. That world doesn't make sense to my generation. We don't want your world. We want a world of our own. The world you gave us isn't secure; it's filled with war and hatred. And you gave us a small religion. Your God isn't big enough to fill our needs. We got a divided God . . . a God divided into small pieces with each person holding on to one piece claiming he's right.

"Look at Gary and me. We were brought up in different beliefs, but both of us have wonderful parents who want the best for us. Did it ever occur to you how confused we are? Gary tells me that he will change and take up my faith because my father is a minister and it would be hard on Dad. And I tell Gary that I will go with him because it would break his parents' hearts if he left the Catholic Church. I brag that my family is broad-minded, that they will understand. We are eating our hearts out. I took instruction from Father Smith and he's the dearest priest who ever lived. But the harder he tried to convince me, the more confused I became. We don't know what to do. Don't you see, Mom, why college isn't important? The only thing that counts is if we can find happiness . . . just a little happiness before the world blows up."

Elsa stared at Susan as if she saw her for the first time. All that had been inside her and Elsa had not known. How wonderful that she had spoken at last! But what could Elsa do about it? How could she make Susan's world right?

"Susan," said Elsa in a sweet voice, "you've given me a lot to think about." She was her old self again and she wanted so much to understand her daughter's deep thoughts. "I never realized how you looked at things or what kind of a world you had to live in. How can we mend our communication lines so we can try to understand each other? There was a time, you know, when we did trust and understand."

The room was very still for a long while. Neither Susan nor Elsa spoke. Each seemed lost in her own thoughts.

Then Elsa spoke in a gentle tone. "I remember a long time ago, Susan, when you were a very litle girl of three or four. We were in New Hampshire in the fall, and we had visited a neighbor's house not far from the parsonage. We were walking the short distance home and you were afraid of the dark and began to cry. It was pitch-black as it can be up there in the fall, and you were scared. I remember how I picked you up in my arms and carried you home. You put your soft cheek against mine and it was wet from tears and your arms went around my neck and you whispered in my ear, 'Mommy, I'm not afraid when you hold me close. Even the dark doesn't scare me.'

"I put you to bed that night and as I stood there looking at you, I was so grateful for you. You looked like a little angel. When you fell asleep, I prayed that I would always be able to carry you through the dark. I don't think I've done so well."

Susan came over to the chair in which Elsa was sitting and put her arms around her mother's neck.

"Don't worry about what I said, Mom. I still need you and if the darkness comes, I'm sure I'll be right back in the shelter of your love again."

"Yes, darling," said Elsa, "There is still a way we can communicate. There is a key and that key is love."

Something special happened that night; a bit of that old feeling between mother and daughter was stirring.

They just think they are so different and so far from us, Elsa thought, but they aren't really. Inside their hearts our children are still little boys and girls crying out in the dark for us to be close to them. They do need us . . . more than ever they need our help in this strange world.

It is a comfort to think like that. It warmed Elsa's soul and lifted her spirits. She would try to understand.

Even if Susan went through with her plan to drop out of college, she would try to understand.

Elsa decided not to tell Mark what Susan had said. I'll wait until it happens, she told herself. Young people often change their minds, but nursing is a fine profession, and Susan would be a beautiful, gentle nurse.

As Christmas drew near, Elsa missed David more than ever.

"Do you think David will remember how beautiful our Christmases in the parsonage have always been?" she asked Mark one night in December. "Do you think he will come home for Christmas?"

She saw the pain in Mark's eyes.

"I hope so, Elsa. It would make Christmas so beautiful if our home were complete again."

But David did not come home, and Gary tried hard to fill his place. He attended a college only twenty-five miles from the village, so he came home almost every weekend. And this year Susan and Gary planned to spend Christmas in the parsonage.

Bernie, too, seemed quite excited about Christmas and he seemed to take in all the preparations. He was always right there with Eric to sample the baking and when the Christmas tree was decorated, his eyes shone like two candles.

"I wish we had a Christmas tree, too," he confided in Eric. "Of course we celebrate Chanukah with gifts, but I love the candles and all the lights on the tree and the piles of packages under it."

117

Eric was happy. This was one time he could shine because of his religious beliefs. He hoped that Bernie would be just a wee bit envious and that he would spend a lot of time in the parsonage on Christmas Eve.

Mrs. Danewich also came to have coffee and sample the Christmas cookies that Elsa had baked. This year there were seventeen different kinds, made from recipes given to Elsa by her Swedish grandmother who had immigrated to America many years ago. Even though her grandmother had been dead for some time, Elsa had never forgotten all the things Grandma had taught her, and Christmas always brought memories of a sweet old woman with a million wrinkles on her dear face.

It was fun for Elsa to entertain Mrs. Danewich. She was a beautiful, intelligent person and Eric loved her.

"The boys are growing up," Mrs. Danewich said, taking another cookie. "It wasn't very long ago that we had to watch them all the time. Now they're so self-sufficient."

"But they're good boys and such pals," smiled Elsa. "How lucky they are to have such a friendship."

"I hope it will last a lifetime."

"We all love Bernie. He has become a part of the parsonage family, just as Eric has a share in your home."

After Mrs. Danewich had gone, Elsa could not help thinking what a lonely little boy David had been. He always chose to play by himself. Then it had been trucks, trains, and airplanes. He would sit for hours completely happy just to have his playthings. Maybe if he had had a friend like Bernie, he would have talked out his anger. But he had always been a loner, and when his disappointments got too heavy, he had just gone off by himself—perhaps even more lonely than he had been before. If only he would come home for Christmas . . .

Elsa sat down in her beautifully decorated living room. Christmas was everywhere. She really did go overboard when it came to preparing for the holidays, but she did love dragging out all the old boxes and transforming the rooms into a real Christmas house. There were candles and Santa Clauses and angels and everything that belonged to Christmas. How she loved it all! And this living room was the prettiest one she had ever had. She sat enjoying the stillness of the house this afternoon. Eric was with Bernie, and Mark was still in his church study. She knew that Mark enjoyed the greens, wreaths, and candles that graced his church. It was Christmas everywhere and if that lonely feeling in her heart hadn't been there, everything would be beautiful.

The sharp jangle of the telephone broke the stillness, and Elsa knew, although she couldn't explain how, that when she answered it, she would hear David's voice.

And it was David! He sounded so near that a big lump formed in her throat and for a moment she couldn't answer.

"Are you there, Mom?" he asked.

"Yes, David! Yes, I'm here and I'm the happiest mother in the whole world. You've given me the gift I wanted most of all . . . to hear your voice."

"Everything is going well, Mom, and I'm fine."

"Are you coming home, David? Can we expect you for Christmas Eve supper?"

"I'm not quite ready to come home yet, Mom. Bear with me a little longer. After bumming around for a while, I came to New Hampshire last fall. It was like coming home. I went to Mr. Swan and told him just how things were with me, and he said you all had stayed here last July for a month. Then he offered me a job at the ski lodge until spring, and I took it. It's a good job and I love it. Maybe when I finish, I'll be home."

"Say that again, David."

"I might be home in the spring."

"Oh, David, you'll never know how happy I am. I'll wait patiently as long as you don't forget."

"You can tell Dad that I called, but don't let on where I am."

"I won't, David. I promise. I know you'll have a wonderful time with the Swans. Merry, merry Christmas, son."

"Merry Christmas, Mom, and I love you."

The telephone clicked. Those were the most emotional words David had ever spoken, and his mother would treasure them in her heart forever.

Elsa sat without moving for a long time. It had been so wonderful to hear David's voice, and he had been so sweet. Perhaps it had been good for him to be away from home. God led in mysterious ways.

When Mark arrived home, he found her still sitting there in the big green velvet chair absorbed in thought. Elsa could not hide her joy; she seemed to sparkle.

"Mark," she said softly, "David called to wish us a Merry Christmas."

Mark stared in disbelief.

"Is he coming home?"

"In the spring, perhaps. He said he had a good job. Isn't that wonderful, Mark? At least we know he's thinking of us. I wish you'd been here, too, so you could have talked to him."

Mark's voice was sad. "If he had wanted to talk to me, he could have called the church, Elsa. But I'm glad he talked to you. We'll be friends again when he returns, and at least we know he's alive and well."

That Christmas was one they would never forget. The whole world seemed new. Snow began to fall early on Christmas Eve and a soft white mantle covered the parsonage garden. Everything dark and ugly was hidden. Before supper Mark drove down to the apartments with some small gifts for each household. Mostly they were things Elsa had baked and wrapped in festive paper. Elsa knew that the snow would have done its work in the north end, too; the apartments would look different in the whiteness. And inside so many of the homes was new paint and paper. Elsa was glad for Mark that it had snowed on Christmas Eve.

That night as the family sat down to the traditional Swedish smörgasbord, they bowed their heads in thankfulness for home and loved ones. Even Mark's prayer seemed very special as he thanked God for His gift of love to the world at Christmas. He thanked God for the people he had been given to love and help, for the stars that shone through the parsonage windows and also cast their light over the apartments, and for those people living in the north end who could look up and see the stars.

When the Cartlings went to bed that night, Elsa's heart was brimming over with joy. She was too happy to go to sleep—happy because David's voice was still ringing in her heart.

"I love you," he had said shyly and quickly—and then hung up. But she would hear those words over and over again and they would give her the strength to wait until the snow was gone and the birds began to build their nests, until the green leaves appeared and the first flowers blossomed. That would be the sign. Then it would not be long until the day she heard footsteps and saw David tall and straight walking up to the front door. Then she would open it and he would be home again and all would be well.

Just a few months now . . . just a few more months.

～ 12

IT HAD NOT been easy for Mark and Elsa to let Susan drop out of college. It was hard for Mark to refrain from demanding that she stay at least until the year was up. And he surely would have done just that if he had not gone through the experience with David. His son had been gone all these months and Mark's heart still ached because of his own thoughtlessness. He certainly did not want to drive Susan away from home, too; nor did he want to drive her into an early marriage. He could not afford to lose her. If becoming a nurse was what his daughter wanted, then he had to let her do it.

Nursing, after all, was a noble profession. Susan would make a fine nurse and patients would adore her. Perhaps her mission was giving comfort to suffering people. Mark had begun to learn that young people knew what they wanted out of life, and when they were sure of their calling, they bypassed everything else to obtain their goal. They were a strong-minded group and nothing that parents had to suggest would change their minds.

Gary seemed deeply settled in college though, and he was doing well. He planned to go into engineering and was looking forward to a good position with a fine salary. He was a smart boy and a real comfort to Mark when he missed David so much. Gary, in his own way, had tried to fill David's place and had made himself very dear to both Elsa and Mark. Gary and Susan would surely find happiness, but there was still plenty of time before they planned to marry as both of them wanted to graduate first. In the meantime, they would have a chance to learn to know each other.

Mark had noticed that Susan and Elsa had become very close since Susan was back home. When Susan had a day off, the two of them usually planned to spend it together—mostly on shopping trips. They seemed to have so much to talk about and laugh about. Mealtimes around the dining-room table had become a focal point to which the whole family looked forward. Never had there been so much fun and chatter as there was now. They all seemed to draw forth the best in each other.

This was the way it should be, Mark philosophized. Parents had to stop panicking when a child stepped out of the pattern drawn for him. Parents had to expect changes to occur and had to be willing to adjust to them. If only David would return home now, everything would be right again.

It was Saturday morning and Mark was in his study waiting for his first appointment. As he looked in his engagement book, he was surprised to find that Gary had made an appointment for counseling at ten o'clock. Why in the world did Gary feel that he had to come to the study? They certainly had plenty of time to slip off alone in the parsonage where Gary was counted as a member of the family. Was it something that concerned Gary so deeply that he wanted to consult a minister?

Gary arrived on time and soon they sat facing each other.

"I know you're wondering why I'm here, Mr. Cartling," Gary began. "I see you so often that I suppose we could have talked during one of my visits. But this is very important to me and I want to approach it in the right way."

"I'm glad you came, Gary," said Mark. "I'm anxious to know what is on your mind. Is it something concerning you and Susan?"

"No, it has nothing to do with us or our different religions this time. I have pushed that way back in my mind since we decided to wait a few years before we are married. I hope by that time we have found a solution to our church problems so we can both live in peace with the Church and ourselves. I can assure you that if we have children, they will never be torn between two beliefs. We do want to have a happy home."

Gary's words pleased Mark. The boy seemed to have a depth that was most unusual in one so young.

"A happy home life, Gary," Mark answered, "is the key to a good life. We create the atmosphere that surrounds our personalities, that makes us bring out the best or worst in those whom we love. If you and Susan can bring out the best in each other, you can't help but find happiness."

"I think we do that! There's no tension when we're together, but I have noticed that people are magnets that draw certain atmospheres from others."

"Love is the keyword. Nothing influences another as much as a person filled with love toward his fellow men."

"Well, I didn't come to talk about love. I came here today to talk about war," said Gary. "You know I've registered for the draft. I've got a student deferment for now, but I do worry about later. If there's a war when I'm finished with school, I have to go. It bothers me; I think about it day and night. How can the world be so unfair, forcing young men to give their lives to such a wretched cause? Even if we're at peace, there's no assurance that it will last. I know why people are rebellious and restless. We want to have a sane world with a future to look forward to. The system as it exists today must go. At school we talk about it and we have some very firey discussions."

"Let's get this straight, Gary. Did you come here to ask me why we have wars or what you should do if you're called upon to serve your own country?"

"To be honest, I don't know exactly what I was planning to say. And I know there's no real answer. I think I just wanted to blow off steam and to help still the restlessness within me when I think of the future. I love Susan so very much and having to go into the service

126

would infringe on our happiness, even if I never have to fight on a battlefield. Perhaps I wanted you to tell me if my thinking is right or wrong or if there is a way to escape learning to kill."

Mark sat silent for a moment. Gary was not the first young man who had come to him with this problem. To guide a young man's thoughts was a sacred mission; to set him right or wrong was a minister's duty for which he was responsible only to God, and Mark had always tried to find a solution.

His voice took on a quality of tenderness as he said, "Gary, there was a time when our young men gave themselves for their country with pride and honor. They answered the call to duty knowing that their country needed them. They were brave and willing. Many who went to battle never returned and sometimes they were buried in foreign soil far from their homeland. Their families were as courageous as they. They mourned, but they never complained. Each mother seemed to know that a son was given to her only as a loan and when his country called, he answered, even if it meant the thick of battle. Today, very few people think dying is noble. We've reached an era when war has lost its glamour and when those who have to go, go sullenly and rebelliously. I can't give you an answer. All I can offer is that mankind has taken one step in the right direction, and the next step will be to outlaw war completely."

"Don't you agree that outlawing war is the right step?"

"Yes, Gary, I do. I would like very much to see an

end to war. But to stop war, we have to stop hate. That is the source of wars; hate is the seed of all evil. One nation alone can't stop war because another would just come to take over his land. Do you understand that? Have you seen what can happen to a small nation that is too weak to resist? It becomes subject to tyranny and the country no longer belongs to the people. This is where America enters. We're a powerful nation and the small, weak ones look to us for help. Where would the small ones be if there were no America?"

"Then you are saying that war is right?"

"No. I'm just saying that to stop war all nations must lay down their arms and learn to respect each other. Gary, suppose you saw a little fellow sitting on the curb swinging a stick, minding his own business, and a big bully suddenly appeared who shoved the little fellow around, broke his stick, and tormented him. If you were as big as that bully, would you help the little fellow or just let the bully do with him what he wanted?"

"You know I'd fight that bully and make sure he left that little fellow alone."

"I knew you'd say that. Well, that seems to be our national situation today. As long as there are bullies who enjoy hurting and tormenting others, our country's young men have to be brave and ready to fight."

"I guess I see that side, too, but I still hope I never have to go out to kill or be killed. You've given me a lot to think about. For the first time I see a reason for young, strong men to serve their country. I'll think about it and one day perhaps I'll know what's right and what's

128

wrong. Thank you, Mr. Cartling. You've become a close friend and I'll be proud to call you my father-in-law."

Long after the door had closed behind Gary, Mark remained deep in thought, forgetting both time and place. His conscience was in an uproar. Had he given Gary the right guidance? Had he made him just a bit taller for his God and his country, or more restless as he tried to tackle the meaning of young manhood in America? Mark hoped and prayed that he had said the right words, words which he could even use to his own son if he ever came asking the same question. They had talked a long time, he and Gary, and his final words to Gary still echoed in his mind just as Gary's answer did.

"Dare to dream big dreams, my boy, and fix your eyes upon a star. Have a goal that you must reach and leave the rest in the hands of God."

Gary had taken Mark's hand and held it firmly.

"Thank you for your help," he had said, looking into Mark's face, his dark eyes filled with a love of life. "I don't know just now how far I am from my goal. I don't know if my dreams will ever become realities or how high my star is. But I do know this—that with men like you and Father Smith in this world we certainly need not be lost or bewildered. You've helped me more than you'll ever know."

The clock on the study wall ticked away the minutes, and when finally there was a knock on the door and Bill Lowell entered, Mark realized that noon had passed and he had not had any lunch. He didn't even feel hungry;

there was still a deep confusion in his heart and an inexplicable restlessness that as a minister he experienced again and again. It seemed to be a by-product of his job.

But now he focused his attention on Bill who was beaming from ear to ear. In his hand he waved a check.

"I just had a caller! Olive sent him to me because you were busy. I've never seen the man before and he didn't say much. He just left this check with a note pinned on it. This ought to make you walk on air."

Mark stared at the bank check—one thousand dollars! At first he thought he had misread the figures, but he was not mistaken. Then he read the note:

Dear Pastor Cartling,
   I have followed with interest your progress in changing the neighborhood on Linden Street. This should help you complete your work. What a fine church you must have which does not just preach the gospel, but lives it.

A Friend

"Bill, this is magnificent! Now we can finish painting the outside of the buildings, and the other money can be used for those extra touches. You know that Elsa and Carol have been dreaming of bright-colored awnings and window boxes filled with red geraniums."

"And pansies!" said Bill. "Carol is bound to plant pansies somewhere on that property. She's crazy about those soft velvety things."

"We'll find a place for them!"

130

Bill smiled. "What a show place Linden Street will be, Mark! I'd almost like to live there myself. How about taking a ride down there now to look it over?"

In a few moments they were in Mark's car driving down toward the north end. It was a pleasant trip. The check provided the encouragement the two ministers needed.

"Those people seem to have changed since we fixed things up," said Bill. "I've even heard the men whistling and the children laughing. There's plenty of room to play now and that swimming pool is a touch of heaven for those kids."

"And I think they've changed inside, too, Bill," said Mark seriously. "Do you still think I'm out of line inviting them to our church?"

"No, I think you were right the whole time, Mark. I'm sure now that some of those people will make fine, faithful church members. The Church has a very special place in the world—a sort of lighthouse in the ocean that guides the ships safely into the harbor. The greatest mission of the Church is to lead the people from darkness to light, to turn their minds to God."

Mark's face beamed as his anxiety diminished.

"Thank you, Bill," he said. "You've been part of this venture and now you've seen results with your own eyes. You've seen people's expressions changing from desperation to hope. And their children are no longer sullen, mistrusting youngsters; they are friendly, open kids. I'm happy. I feel like celebrating. How about asking the girls out to dinner tonight?"

"Fine! After we have inspected our property-of-good-will, we'll surprise them."

"Perhaps we'd better stop and phone first. They might not appreciate the offer if they've already cooked dinner."

Just as they had anticipated, their wives were ready and willing for a night on the town.

As they pulled up in front of the apartments and were admiring their work, one of the tenants, Mrs. Alexson, spotted them and walked up to the car.

"Hello," she said. "You haven't seen my finished apartment. If you pay me a visit, I promise you a cup of coffee and some newly baked cupcakes. And wait until you see my new kitchen!"

Mark and Bill followed Mrs. Alexson up two flights of stairs and were ushered into her kitchen, which had been painted a soft yellow. There was a new white sink and a shiny stove, and crisp new curtains draped the windows. The place was as bright as a summer day."

"How do you like it since it's been fixed up?" she asked eagerly.

"It's magnificent, Mrs. A!" said Mark. "You certainly have added many touches to make it the prettiest kitchen for miles around."

"I can't believe it's really mine. Everything used to be such a mess! But I think you've brought us all good luck. Why, I've even been given a raise."

"It has been worthwhile and I'm happy for all of you. But most of all, I'm happy to see that you've been coming to church on Sunday mornings."

132

"Well, that's the least we can do for you. I don't know how we can ever repay you for the new start you've given us. We've even organized a group down here to keep this place beautiful. We've elected inspectors to make rounds to keep everything in order."

The coffee tasted good and sitting around the kitchen table was cozy and informal. Mrs. Alexson was so proud and happy about her home that even her personal appearance had changed. Discouraged and lonely before, she now bubbled over with things to tell. And she was just one of the people. Most of their stories were similar. Now they worked to help spread joy and beauty, all because someone cared. Mrs. Alexson's three-room apartment had been done over entirely and after the last few apartments were finished, every tenant would have new surroundings.

The next month the painting of the exterior of the buildings was completed. The first coat had been put on by the church's young people, but the second coat was done by a professional. The white buildings were now surrounded by green lawns, and a new sidewalk and trees had been furnished by the city. An empty lot, once full of junk and trash, had been hard-topped to provide a parking lot. Everywhere there was order, and as money kept coming in, more and more luxuries were added.

The newspaper had sent a photographer after the painting was completed and the newly decorated apartments made the front page with the headline:

After that more and more contributions came through the mail, and before May was ended the awnings were up and there were window boxes filled with red geraniums, and pansies had been planted in urns by the front entrance. Mark's happiness knew no bounds. The completion was more than he had expected, more than he had even dared to dream.

One evening Father Smith and Mark drove down to Linden Street. For a few moments they just sat there and looked at the apartments.

"I can't believe it, Mark. It really is finished! If this has not been God's work, I don't know what has. If every church would undertake a small project and a small group of people started to transform both material and soul, what a change would come over our world."

"I think it has to be done that way if the world is going to change. But it must be done for the glory of God."

For a long time they sat in silence, both of them thinking of the people they had worked with, the tears they had seen, the stories they had been told, the long hours of counseling, and their own patience in showing God to those who did not believe He existed. That was a worthwhile task. They both agreed that nothing had given them more satisfaction.

Father Smith went home with Mark for a cup of coffee in the parsonage and a taste of Elsa's newly baked buns. Their conversation was like music. How close they felt in their fellowship, how rich in their friendship. And this was only the beginning, Mark hoped, a beginning of peace on earth and god will toward all men.

If only his church would fall into step now. If only its members would welcome the people from Linden Street and make them feel like a part of the church. As yet none had become members. Mark longed for that to happen even though he feared the results. For as peace had come to the apartments, war was starting in the once-peaceful church on the hill. Where would it lead? Where would it end?

As Mark retired that night his heart was troubled. He wished he had the wisdom to solve this problem, a problem that could grow into an ugly situation if it were not stopped in time.

~ 13

ELSA WAS SURE that there had never been a more excited
boy than her Eric. His eyes shone and his voice had a
lilt every time he talked about a certain coming event.
A great day was due in his friend Bernie's life. The
twelfth of May this year Bernie was to celebrate his Bar
Mitzvah. Of course the Cartlings had been invited and
Eric, as Bernie's best friend, was to be a very special
guest. The invitations had been engraved cards which
included a reception immediately following the service.
Elsa knew this was to be a buffet supper for at least two
hundred persons.

"This is the biggest event in a Jewish boy's life, Mom,"
chanted Eric, as he sat at the kitchen table watching
Elsa bake cookies. "After the twelfth of May, Bernie
will be a man and everyone will respect him. I wish we
had something like that in our church!"

"We do, Eric! We do! We have confirmation and

136

dedication and some youngsters are baptized at this age."

"That's nothing, Mom, compared to what Bernie will have. He is going to read from the Torah . . . and that is the most sacred thing that can happen to a boy."

"I know it will be wonderful Eric, and we'll all enjoy it. I'm glad we were invited. But don't let this one occasion outshine your own faith, dear. Someday when you are a little older, your dad will explain all about the Bar Mitzvah and then you can ask him lots of questions about the difference in religions—why we are Protestants and most of all, why we are Christians. There's so much to know, Eric. But now, let's just be glad for Bernie and enjoy every moment of his big night."

Elsa discussed it with Mark later.

"I can't understand it, Mark. Bernie's synagogue means so much more to Eric than his own church. I'm almost at a loss for words when I talk to him about it. He has Bernie and the Jewish faith on a pedestal. I just hope they never tumble down."

"Well, it's an awesome occasion when a boy's closest friend celebrates his Bar Mitzvah. The novelty of it is fascinating, I suppose. To tell the truth, I'm excited about it myself. I've never attended one before either. As for our younger son, we'll just have to guide him the best way we can and try to make him see the beauty in our Christmas and Easter celebrations. I think we have a great deal of beauty and dignity in our form of worship."

137

Elsa sat quietly for a moment, thinking it over.

"It isn't the beauty that we lack, Mark. I think what we lack is the color and tradition. Eric can see pictures of Bernie's faith. Everything that happens is accompanied by a picture from Old Testament times. And Eric loves to use the Hebrew names for the Jewish holidays. The names themselves are fascinating and colorful, don't you think? Let's see, there's Shema and Yom Kippur and, oh, so many others."

Elsa was thinking about Eric again that night as she sat alone in the living room, watching the last glow of the logs in the fireplace and listening to the stillness of the parsonage. What a unique friendship Eric and Bernie had! How honest and frank they were as they discussed and compared their different churches, and how much admiration there was on both sides. If only adults could be like that—trying to understand instead of condemning so quickly. How much grownups had to learn from children.

When the great day finally arrived, Eric, dressed in his best dark blue suit, new shoes, and new tie, was glowing with excitement. He had asked especially for new clothes.

"Everything Bernie is wearing will be new," he had explained to his parents.

But Elsa had insisted that his suit was good enough; however, there were some things he could have new.

"Remember that it's Bernie, not you, who is celebrating his Bar Mitzvah," she had reminded her son.

138

It was hard to convince Eric that he was not "family." He insisted that he wanted to sit in the front pew in the synagogue.

"That pew is reserved for the family, Eric," said Mark in a firm voice.

It was almost too firm, thought Elsa. But Mark was right. They certainly could not march up to the front pew as a family, though they certainly should sit together.

They finally agreed on the third pew from the front, and from there Eric was sure he could see and hear everything that took place.

Eric sat spellbound. His eyes never left Bernie's face. A guest rabbi, Bernie's uncle, led the ceremony. Rabbi Danewich sat at the back of the platform on one side of Bernie. On the other side sat Bernie's grandfather, who had come all the way from Arizona. Bernie's eyes were shining and his whole face glowed. When the proper moment came, the rabbi slowly pulled open the curtain and took out the sacred Torah, then turned to Bernie, his father, and his grandfather who stood in front of it waiting anxiously. First the Torah was handed to the grandfather, who in his turn handed it over to Bernie's father, who tenderly placed it in Bernie's hands. What a moment that was! A hush fell over the synagogue and Bernie, placing the Torah on the pulpit, began to read in Hebrew.

Eric could barely stay in his seat in his pride over Bernie. Bernie read passage after passage. Some were translated into English. Some the congregation took part in. The service was long and when it was finished, the Torah was returned to its holy chamber and the Danewich family marched out. To Elsa the service had been beautiful and meaningful, much more than she had anticipated. She was glad they had attended as she, too, had gained a deeper understanding of the Jewish way of worshiping God. She was deeply impressed.

Soon they were at the reception where a receiving line had been formed. They all shook hands with Bernie and his family. Eric brought his gift—an instamatic camera wrapped in gold paper—and laid it on the pile of gifts. In addition to the gifts there was also a basket of envelopes.

Eric had whispered to Elsa, "Mom, did you see all those gifts? And the envelopes, too . . . there's money in them! Bernie will not only be a man; he'll be a rich man."

Elsa patted Eric's head. "Good for Bernie," she whispered. "When Christmas comes, you'll get your pile of gifts. And you are a man now just as much as Bernie is, even if you didn't have a ceremony."

The reception was elegant—lots of food and music and happy people. It was over much too soon.

"Is Bernie really a man now?" Eric asked as they entered the parsonage.

"I suppose he is if that is what this ceremony signifies," answered Elsa, "but we'll consider you a young man, too, Eric, if you act like one. I'm sure Bernie has many challenges to meet just as you do. How you meet them indicates how grown up you are."

That night when Elsa went into Eric's room to kiss him good night, it suddenly dawned on her that no matter how big Eric tried to be, he was still a very little boy in many ways. As she kissed him lightly on the top of the head, he flung his arms around her neck in a strangle hold.

"Do you know what, Mom?" he said in her ear.

"No, what, Eric?"

"I love you and I think you're beautiful!"

Elsa felt so good that in her heart she hoped this part of Eric would always remain a little boy. Not many years ago David had been Eric's age and although he had always been more shy in demonstrating his feelings, there were times when he, too, had covered her face with wet kisses and spoken words that she would remember forever.

Being a mother was a bittersweet thing—seeing your children grow up and go away as David had without even a farewell. David had been gone so long now without a note or a sign since that one phone call. She had been so sure he would return in early spring. And he *had* mentioned it on Christmas Eve. 'I might be home in the spring,' he had said. But spring would be fading into summer soon.

Oh, David, David, her heart cried. Life will never be right again until you return to us.

The temptation to call the Swans in New Hampshire had been great sometimes. She had stood with her finger ready to dial the number, but always she had stopped herself in time. It must be David's decision, she had told herself. He must return of his own free will because he wanted to come home.

The last day of May turned into a beautiful balmy spring night. Elsa had worked in the garden most of the day and she was tired as she sat in the family room glancing at the evening paper. Although it was warm, she had thrown a few sticks of wood in the fireplace. This would probably be the last fire until fall, she thought. Eric had gone to bed and Mark had been called to the hospital to attend one of his older church members who had had a heart attack. Susan was on duty at the hospital, so Elsa was alone with her own thoughts. Mark had been gone two hours; there was no need to wait up for him. If the person were dying, Mark would stay at the hospital most of the night. As soon as the fire had burned itself out, she would take a bath and go to bed. She had worked very hard in the garden today to set out so many new little flower plants and her muscles ached from stretching.

Suddenly she sat up straight on the sofa. Someone seemed to be moving around on the back porch. Of course it could be her imagination. There certainly was nothing to be afraid of; there had never been a prowler around the parsonage for as long as they had lived there, and the back door was locked and chained. But ... there it was again, the sound of footsteps outside the door. A strange uneasiness filled her; she had better stay up until Mark returned. She hoped it would be soon. Elsa admitted to herself that she was afraid!

Then came a knock! At first it was faint, then a little

louder. A chill went through her body. Who could be at the back door of the parsonage at this time of the night? It was already past ten o'clock.

Forcing herself to be brave, she walked to the door. "Who is there?" she called out.

"It's me, Mom," came a voice from outside. "It's David."

In a second she had flung open the door and there he stood. David. Her lost son—David. He looked much the same, although he was thinner and his hair had been allowed to grow down to his neck. But it was really David—not just a vision. David had come home while it was still May.

In another moment she was embracing him, holding him fast as if he might disappear again.

"David, David!" was all she could say.

They walked into the kitchen, her arm in his, and she realized he had grown taller. His clothes needed pressing and his shoes were muddy.

"Dad is at the hospital," she said, just to say something. For just a moment she felt that she had forgotten how to communicate.

"I knew he was out," David answered. "I've been in the garden a long time. I saw him drive off."

"You didn't want to come in while he was here?"

"I just feel strange about facing him. I'm still bitter, I suppose. It took me a long time to work up the courage to knock on the door even when I knew you were alone. I've been gone so long."

"But we've waited so for you, David. Life hasn't been

right without you. I hope you feel how welcome you are."

"I'll be fine, Mom. Don't worry about me. But right now all I want is to take a shower and go to bed."

"Your room is ready and waiting for you. Go take your shower and I'll bring some hot chocolate and sandwiches."

David hurried up the stairs and Elsa stood there for a moment with her hand over her heart. She had restrained herself to the uttermost. Her first impulse had been to hold her son close and cover him with kisses. But David would not have liked that. Emotional displays always upset him, so she had acted against her feelings to please him. The most important thing now was to make him feel happy, but it was hard to be a mother and not show her true feelings. Yet this she must learn if she was to keep David close.

It did not take him long to shower and get into bed. Elsa brought him his snack and sat beside him while he ate. Then she turned out the light, left the room, and went downstairs to wait for Mark. Suddenly she was wide awake and all fatigue she had felt was gone.

It was midnight when Mark returned. At first she considered keeping her news until morning, but Mark knew something had happened.

"What's wrong, Elsa?" he asked as he sat at the kitchen table with a glass of milk. "You look so strange."

She could hold back no longer. In a moment she was in his arms, sobbing her heart out.

"What's happened, Elsa?" he asked tenderly. "Something must be very wrong."

144

Elsa looked up at her husband then with tears still running down her cheeks.

"Nothing is wrong, dear. Everything is so right—so very, very right. Our David is upstairs sleeping in his own bed. He came home tonight, Mark! He's back with us again!"

"I must go to him, Elsa—or shouldn't I? Do you think David wants to see me?"

"He's sound asleep now. He looked so tired and worn out. Why don't you wait until morning, Mark? But we can just peek in so you can see for yourself that he really is there."

Together they mounted the stairs, softly pushing open the door to David's room, just as they used to when the children were babies. David was sound asleep with only the top of his hair sticking out of the bed clothes. Mark closed the door after a moment and stood outside it with his head bowed as if in prayer. Mark and Elsa spoke very little that night. It was a precious time because the family unit had been restored. A day could not have ended more perfectly, and as Elsa fell asleep, the soft music of love and home and togetherness was her lullaby.

The meeting in the morning between father and son was joyful. There was not an embrace, but a firm handclasp. They were both just a little restrained, but both knew that past hurts and mistakes had been forgiven. That same day when Elsa went down to the basement, she found the door to David's laboratory wide open. On his workbench was a note and a crisp ten dollar bill. Elsa read the note, and foolish tears ran down her cheeks as her heart warmed again at the wonder of love.

Son,
   Forgive your thoughtless dad for taking away your freedom and causing you grief. I understand now and never again will I object to your following your heart's desire.

This was surely a new beginning with laughter and fun in a happy parsonage. Little by little David opened his heart and talked about the months he had been away. Elsa attempted to piece together what had taken place while David was gone. As nearly as she understood it, he had at first hitch-hiked from one place to another, sleeping in cheap places, looking for a day's work. He did manage to get enough jobs to keep himself alive after his own money was gone. Many times he had felt like returning home, but he had never weakened. He had been lonely and bitter. Then he had thought of New Hampshire and their old family friends, the Swans. David said he would never forget how warmly they had received him into their home as if he had been a son. All winter he had helped Mr. Swan in his ski lodge, and he had told the older man of his bitterness and loneliness. Mr. Swan had listened and tried to understand. Since Mr. Swan had also been the lay preacher in the church after Mark left, he let David help him with many things there, too. David had even become the leader of the young people's group, and had become very attached to this work.

146

"Oh, don't think I wasn't lonely for home and family," David confided. "But I couldn't forgive Dad. It seemed that he had snuffed out the real me and left just a shell. Then one night Mr. Swan and I had a long talk and he tried to make me understand a parent's viewpoint and the problems parents faced. He said that very often they made mistakes, too. That softened me up a bit and I began to toy with the idea of going home. The Swans encouraged me and one day I packed up my belongings and hitch-hiked to Robendale-by-the-Sea. I'm glad now that I came home. I think I've learned a lot and I feel as though I've really grown up."

Elsa treasured his words. It did her heart good to see how close David and Mark were growing. She couldn't help but think of all those parents who had lost their children, not through death, but through misunderstanding and bitterness. Next to heaven came a happy home, and it was up to each family member to keep it that way. And the only tie that could really hold them together was made up of trust and love and understanding.

The Cartling family was whole again! The birds were singing in the garden and the flowers were blooming. Elsa could set five places at the table when Susan was home, and sometimes six when Gary came to visit. And she never tired of cooking mouth-watering meals and seeing them eaten. Life was good again.

There had never been a happier spring, she thought as she walked among the tulips and lilies-of-the-valley. The lilacs were blooming as they never had before and

147

soon the roses would begin to bud and fill the garden with their fragrance.

David had lost almost a whole year of high school, and he would have to repeat it in the fall, but that would keep him home a little longer and college would come soon enough. Elsa had no objections.

~ 14

IT WAS FINISHED! The project that Mark had started had been completed on this very day in June, almost three years to the day he and his family had moved to Robendale-by-the-Sea. A once-unsavory part of the village was gone. Many willing hands had been extended to make it beautiful and livable. People had labored without pay, spending long hours, sometimes after a day at work, and had given generously of their money to hasten the completion of the work. Newsmen and photographers from the local paper had been there and had taken a number of pictures showing the "before" and "after." And the white church on the hill and its ministers had been given full credit for the miracle of transformation. The congregation should have been proud and had this been the case, Mark's happiness would have been complete. But this was not so. The church members were angry and their anger was focused on a

149

group of people who had found their way to the oldest church in town and had begun to feel at home there. Every Sunday morning they appeared in their shabby clothes, some carelessly dressed, easily noticed among the well-dressed, well-mannered, cultured members. They were not wanted.

"Why?" came the cry. Why do they by-pass so many smaller churches and take the bus across town to attend this church?

The church members were neither hostile nor friendly. They kept their distance in a cool, polite manner, hoping the intruders would take the hint and not request membership. But the apartment people did not seem to notice. They came to listen to the Reverend Mr. Cartling and to enjoy his preaching. They seemed to hang on his every word. It was his hand they wanted to shake and his welcome and smile they were looking for. To them he was a liberator, releasing them from dullness and dirt into life and beauty. The least they could do to repay him was to attend his church.

Mark knew that one day something would blow up. If he himself was to survive, he would have to find a number of leading members to stand at his side. The sin he had committed was the social sin of bringing into God's Church the poor and undesirable, giving them equal status.

For this reason Mark could not include the church in celebrating the completion of his project. Ordinarily there would have been a dedication service by the church, but instead his plans were for a community ceremony. First there was to be an open-house night in the apartments. Mark had requested that every household keep lights on and open doors for people who wanted to see what really had happened in this part of town. Then there would be a festive evening in the parsonage garden where all would take part. This planning he had left to Elsa who, in turn, had recruited Carol Lowell as her committee and her whole family as workers.

The weather that night could not have been more ideal. A full moon shone brightly and thousands of stars twinkled in the night sky. David and Eric had strung colored lights all over the garden and had placed special lights among the shrubs and bushes. Tall torches flamed round the long tables covered with delicious things to eat. A kind electrician had volunteered his services and had done all the wiring as his contribution. Eric and Bernie had made a huge cardboard egg, which they had covered with gold paper and decorated with ribbons and flowers. In the top they had cut a slit so that donations could be put in for any repairs that might be needed in the future to keep up the appearance of the apartments. The boys had worked long and hard on their project and with a little help from Bernie's mother, the egg was a beautiful sight to behold. It stood on its own round marble table and the boys were to be in full charge of it.

Elsa and Carol had arranged a baking party the week before and the baked goods were placed in a town-owned freezer until the evening arrived. They had advertised in the local paper and the response had been tremendous. Women had flocked in to help, bringing their own ingredients and baking their favorite cakes, cookies, and pastries. The last day they made sandwiches, both fancy and plain, to suit all who would attend the party. And, of course, there was coffee in big urns, and gallons and gallons of punch. Susan and Gary were on the welcome committee and in charge of the guestbook. It was the party of parties, a night that the town would never forget.

"We have enough refreshments to feed an army!" Elsa informed Mark as the hour approached. "And the fanciest baked creations that I've ever seen."

"Wonderful, Elsa! Just wonderful!" beamed Mark. Never in his life had a plan blossomed in such beauty and abundance. This really would be a party never to be forgotten—the crowning touch to all the work and preparation that had gone into it.

Just before dusk Elsa decorated the tables with enormous bouquets of fresh flowers. Each table was covered with a colored cloth and with the lights on the garden looked like fairyland. Soon people began to come, hundreds and hundreds of them. The whole town seemed to be moving in the direction of the parsonage on this night and the work of greeting and serving began.

Eric and Bernie were ardent solicitors for the golden egg and no one escaped. Donations large and small fell into it. Eric was the keeper of the egg, but Bernie was the contact man. His job was to round up the people and direct their attention to the importance of the egg.

He was just the right person for no one could resist his big brown eyes and his smile.

Mark was happy to see Mr. and Mrs. Rollins present —home again from their trip around the world.

Mr. Rollins shook Mark's hand, saying, "You've done a fine job, Mark! I couldn't believe my eyes when I saw those apartments. We took a spin down there before we came. What a change! But I still have my doubts that the place will stay that way. I am anxious to see how long your work will last. Those people, as I told you, don't know how to live in clean surroundings."

"Then we must teach them," said Mark with a smile. "I won't consider the project finished until the people are in harmony with their surroundings. That's my job and I'm working on it."

Rollins shook his head and took his wife's arm. They helped themselves to all the goodies and then Bernie ushered them to the egg, holding on to Mr. Rollins' arm so he would not escape. Eric reported later to Mark that Mr. Rollins had contributed a fifty-dollar bill. Mark attributed that generosity to either a change of heart or a guilty conscience.

The egg filled rapidly as the townspeople came and went. The boys' urging was constant. "Even a quarter will help," was their slogan. But the wallets came out and mostly silent money filled the egg. The boys figured that by the time the party was over there would be a couple of thousand dollars in it. It would make a nice cushion for Linden Street.

It was close to eleven o'clock when the last guests

left. The food was cleared away, but the real cleaning up was left until morning. The committee was ready to drop from exhaustion and Elsa and Mark collapsed to a well-earned rest.

Mark awoke early the next morning. He was wide awake, reliving in his mind the wonderful success of the garden party. Quickly he left his bed, dressed casually in sweater and slacks, and drove to Linden Street. He didn't have to go down there; he just wanted to sit there for a while, feeling grateful for the beauty and freshness of this June morning.

Of course, these north-end people would always be his friends and a part of him would belong to them as long as he served in the village. They needed his guidance now and his inspiration to dare to dream and discover their hidden talents. The apartments seemed to be still asleep as the first rays of the sun fell on the light green awnings and bright red geraniums. Everything spoke of order and peace. Evergreens graced the front entrances and the trees on the tree belt, although still small, would, in a few years, give shade and beauty. This is a treasure chest, Mark thought, with all those dear people inside who meant so much to him.

How much he and Elsa had shared with these folks. They had stood by them through struggles and sorrows, weaknesses and confusion. Many nights Mark had sat in some shabby apartment, trying to dry the tears of a frustrated wife with an alcoholic husband. There had been times when he had had to protect a woman against abuse. There had been the dope addicts, too—not many, mostly teen-agers starting off on the wrong road. They had not solved every problem, but they had come a long way together. Many nights Elsa had helped sick children whose mothers had had to go to work. They had spent much time here, but it was good work and surely work that God expected of his servants. Mark had no regrets and he would keep it up as long as he was needed.

The apartments seemed to stir and the pleasant aroma of coffee drifted out into the early morning air. Music could be heard and the sound of adult voices and children's laughter. The harmonious sounds indicated a happy beginning to the new day.

Mark said a silent prayer for each of them, tucking them into his heart as he drove off toward the ocean, now glittering in the early sunlight. The water was calm today and its blueness combined both water and sky. Mark removed his shoes to walk on the damp beach sand. Over his head a few seagulls screeched, spreading their wide wings, their eyes searching the water for their breakfast. Mark's heart was overflowing with good will, fulfillment, and peace. This morning nothing would disturb him. He even felt he had the right to glow at the thought of the blessings that had finally come to this town. His cup was full to overflowing. God was good and His goodness was everywhere.

The noise of a car caught his attention. He looked up to see Father Smith's car parking beside his own. Mark hurried to meet him.

"What brings you out so early this morning, Father John?" he called out.

The priest smiled brightly. "I didn't expect to find

you here, Mark. I was sure you'd still be resting up from last night. My, that was some party!"

"I felt pretty peppy this morning, really ready to go. So I drove down to take another look at the apartments. Then I felt the need for the stillness of the beach."

"A fine place to meditate! I often come here myself in the morning. I sit and look out over God's great ocean and consider the vastness of His power and it brings me peace."

"How about walking down the beach with me? The sand is damp so you'd better take off your shoes. Walking barefoot in the sand is good for the soul."

"I think you've sold me on the idea, Mark. I don't know how proper it is for a priest to walk around barefoot, but it sounds good, so I'll join you."

They walked silently on the sandy beach, each thinking his own thoughts, remembering the months they had worked together for the betterment of the community. They remembered problems they had solved. But most of all, they thought of the brotherly feeling they had for each other, their mutual admiration and respect for each other's opinions. They knew their friendship would last for a lifetime.

Father Smith stopped and scanned the ocean where a small fishing boat was drifting idly.

"Mark," he said, placing his hand on Mark's shoulder. "You are still a young man and have life ahead of you. I've almost completed my earth years—to the best of my ability, I hope. There's much I know and much I don't know. But this I have learned—that if you ask God for a field to work in, He will give it to you. You and I each have our own section to work in the Almighty's great field, but there's plenty to keep us busy. He is always short of laborers."

"Yes, I know. He gave me a field that was pretty hard to till. But the seed is growing now, and I hope to His glory."

"Yes, and you will find another field soon. There's no end to them."

"I guess that each one brings a little more harmony into the world. If only the whole world would find peace!"

"It will come, Mark! It will come in God's own time. His clock is set and the hour might be nearer than we think."

They walked back to their cars, put on their shoes, and parted with a handshake, as warm and firm as the friendship that bound them together.

The day's work was waiting. Each minute was crowded with new tasks. Mark felt especially good after having talked with Father Smith, who always spoke with such wisdom. He was truly a great man. They did work in different fields, but they both served the same Master, and their call was to help a lost generation find their God. People everywhere were bewildered, seeking peace, searching for a purpose in life, often missing their goal because they were on the wrong road.

In the beginning God created the trees and flowers

and grass and gave them the ability to produce seeds that they in their turn might bring forth new trees and flowers and grass. The power to reproduce was there so that what God had created would never die. In people, too, God had planted the seed to regenerate life, but in them He had also planted the seeds to produce good or evil. The future of the new world depended on what seeds the fading generation had been sowing. Good or evil—how important that was to mankind. And there was a kingdom of God implanted in each living soul—a kingdom to be taken or rejected, to be found or to be lost.

As Mark drove home he pondered his own power to think and feel. The God that had created his brain with which to think had also created his soul with which to feel and his heart with which he could return a portion of himself to his Maker. If only Mark could broadcast this so that people would understand God and come into the light of His love where they might find themselves sons of God, heirs to the kingdom someday to return to earth.

Back in the driveway of the parsonage, Mark looked out over the garden. As beautiful as it had seemed last night with the colored lights and the moon and the stars, much of it now seemed cluttered up. The façade of beauty was gone in the daylight, and until it was cleaned up, it was no longer lovely. But it would not take long to restore its original beauty once the family woke up and started setting in order. It was a challenge that would easily be met and soon it would be Elsa's beautiful garden again. So it was with God's work. The challenge to restore was there; all it lacked were the workers to take up the challenge.

A minister—God's servant—seemed to have many jobs—the keeper of the wall, the watchman of the night, the crier of the town, the bearer of good tidings on the mountaintops. These tidings Mark willingly proclaimed. If only the world would stand still long enough to listen and follow the direction to a new life which would never end.

~ 15

IF ELSA CARTLING lived to be a hundred years old, she would never forget the night of the Board meeting in the parsonage. It would haunt her to the end of her days. What went on in that meeting had shattered her high standards of religion and she would always find it difficult to believe that church members could have disgraced themselves by sinking so low. The evening had started out normally; Mark and Elsa had looked forward to opening their home to these important members of the church. Committee meetings were often held in the parsonage and Elsa specialized in the refreshments she served. Tonight she had made delicious apple pies to be topped with ice cream, a favorite dessert of most men, which she had served shortly after everyone had arrived. Everyone had seemed in his best humor, and Mr. Rollins, the Chairman of the group, smiling and gracious, complimented Elsa on her baking.

Bill Lowell had brought Carol along to keep Elsa company, and they had retreated to the family room after clearing away the dishes. Elsa was both glad and sad that Carol had been there—glad because she had had someone to cling to when the voices began to rise, and sad because Carol was so young to go through such an ordeal.

The meeting had been called to deal with the many matters the Board usually tended to, but early in the discussion the subject of the newly renovated apartments had been introduced by Mr. Rollins, who praised the project and the fine work that had been done. Elsa was sure that Mark was as surprised at the words as she was.

"You have done an admirable piece of work, Mark," he had said. "The local paper was generous in their praise for our church, but we know we do not deserve the credit. You were the one who went ahead with the project in spite of our cool support. We did not rally behind you in the beginning, but now we know it was a good move. In fact, we have set an example for the whole country. I want you to know that I have taken a good look at the work and it is superb!"

Elsa had been pleased for Mark. Receiving such recognition from his chief opponent was a real victory, or so it seemed. Elsa and Carol decided to listen after that to hear what other comments might be made.

"Mark," came another voice, "I think we have created a little gold mine. Not only have you transformed that ugly slum into an attractive neighborhood, but you've made it considerably more valuable. Soon we'll be able to look for a greater income from that project."

Mark's deep, firm voice reached the family room

quite clearly, and Elsa knew in her heart how much emotion he was holding back in order to sound calm and collected.

"Certainly not!" he said firmly. "I am humbly grateful for your praise, but we just cannot raise the rent of those apartments. The people themselves did the work without pay, and the money we used did not come from our church. It came from charitable organizations and private donations. You certainly are not seriously thinking that our church should profit from it?"

The women could hear a number of nervous coughs, and then the clearing of a throat, and the same voice spoke again.

"I don't mean that we should levy a twenty-five-dollar increase in rent just now. But in a month or two, we can start increasing the rent a little each month until we reach the right sum. By gosh, they are almost luxury apartments now and we'll never have to worry about having them stand vacant."

"But," insisted Mark stubbornly, "the people who are living there now have lived through those years of dirt and misery when we did nothing to improve their dwellings. They lived there because the rent was cheap. They can't afford to pay any more. A higher rent would force them to move out." Mark's voice was really angry now. "I just want you all to know that as long as I am serving this church, the rents will never go up."

Another voice was heard, a high-pitched, sarcastic voice which Elsa recognized as belonging to Mr. Rollins' good friend Emil Haynes.

162

"I wouldn't talk so uppity if I were you, Mark Cartling. Even if what you accomplished is commendable, you did it on the church's time. The hours you spent down there in the slum were paid for by us. And let me remind you of another thing—ministers who oppose authority in this church never stay long."

"Now, now, gentlemen," came another voice. "Hold on. Let's not begin to quarrel. I'd suggest we get back to the business we came here to discuss in the first place."

"He must be an ally," whispered Elsa to Carol.

The living room was deathly silent for a moment; then someone else spoke up.

"But this is church business, too, and there are some things that I think should be brought out in the open. I don't think our pastor is aware of the resentment caused by these strange people he has brought into the sanctuary on Sunday mornings. They look like a bunch of hoodlums."

A storm of loud angry voices broke in full fury and Mark became the target for a cruel tongue lashing. Elsa's heart almost broke for him and there were tears in Carol's eyes.

Then Bill Lowell's calm, strong voice said, "I want to come to Mark's defense. Let me set every one of you straight on one fact. Those people come to church from the north end on Sunday because they want to come. Mark is a hero to them and they are showing their gratitude to both the pastor and the church by attending. I'm sure they haven't the slightest idea that

163

their attendance is doing Mark harm. How could they understand that they are not wanted in a church?"

Another unpleasant voice interrupted. "They're not our kind of people. They'd never be happy with us, sharing in the social activities of the church. They just don't fit in! For hundreds of years this church has served a cultured, dignified congregation. The community has always held us in esteem. Why, if we accept these people, who knows what kind of person will come next? We don't want or need a minister who plans to change our traditions."

Now Mr. Rollins spoke again. This time his voice was thick and angry.

"It's convenient that the two ministers can support each other. But I'm sure that there is more involved than the attendance of these people at Sunday worship. They must have been encouraged to come or they wouldn't show up in droves as they do."

"That's true," said Mark. "I have encouraged them to come just as I encourage others to attend our church. It's a minister's job. The Protestants come to us, and Father Smith is taking care of the Catholics. How could I have known that the church I am serving doesn't think the poor need God. You are welcome to put the whole blame on me, but I want you to know that I love those people and that it thrills me to see them sitting there on Sunday mornings. I don't see their shabby clothing; I see only their shining faces."

Elsa had tried to close her mind to all the angry words that followed, but they could not be ignored completely.

All those accusations against her husband hurt her as did the jeers and the sarcastic remarks. She wondered how Mark held his peace and kept from throwing them out bodily. She felt that God must have already deserted these men who were judging, shouting, and trampling His name under their feet. Elsa couldn't remember a sadder night, but in retrospect she began to realize how great the tension must have built up against Mark. The church people were bitter and bewildered, and they couldn't understand why they should have to mingle with the illiterate poor.

The door had slammed behind the men as they left the parsonage and she was sure that Mark had neither the chance nor the inclination to be a gracious host.

When Mark and Bill joined Elsa and Carol, the men's faces showed signs of the strain they had undergone. They had very little to say as they sank down into the comfortable chairs, and for the first time that night, seemed to relax. They sat in silence for a long time, and Elsa went to the kitchen to warm the coffee. When conversation finally started, each tried to raise the others' gloom and frustration, but no matter how they tried, the talk kept returning to the tragic meeting.

"I've never attended a meeting like that before," said Bill. "Why, it was as if the very devil himself was loose."

"I'm sure he was!" answered Mark sadly. "One thing was certainly made crystal clear to me. They do hate the apartment people."

"Mark," said Bill, "it has just come to me how much

my views have changed since we started working on this project. I can't believe, for the life of me, that a church can call itself Christian and believe that its congregation is a chosen people, that only the rich and cultured have a right to worship there."

"Oh," said Elsa, "I don't think those men represent the heart of the church. There's a fine group of plain, good people in our church who love the poor and needy. This was just Mr. Rollins' crew and I'm sure that not one of them would be on that Board if he did not have Mr. Rollins' approval."

"You mean," Mark added, "that each one must dance to his pipe."

Carol's face was ashen. "Perhaps," she suggested sweetly, "when they get home, they'll think things over and call to apologize."

Mark smiled. "I wish I could share your faith in mankind, Carol, but those men are hard as nails."

"What will happen now?" wondered Bill.

"Only God knows." Mark sighed. "But one thing is certain; they're not going to raise that rent while I'm here."

"How can you stop them, Mark?" asked Bill. "The church is the landlord."

"I can't see how our church can ever return to normal," moaned Elsa. "How tragic that there had to be a night like this."

"Oh, the whole affair will blow over in a while," said Mark, trying to make his voice light. "These things do happen in churches everywhere and even worse things. I just have never served a church where it's happened

166

to me. The other churches I have served have been less explosive!"

"It makes me wonder if it's worth it," said Carol. "Perhaps you should get out of the ministry before you get in too deep, Bill."

Bill moved closer to his wife.

"Come now, dear," he said tenderly. "You aren't telling me to run away from the first storm, are you? Because I've seen something ugly I'm more determined to stay fast. I've learned a lot tonight. This might have been part of the lesson I have to learn."

"Good for you, Bill," said Mark. "I'm proud of you. One day you will be a great minister and Carol will be standing right along side of you. I know you are both made of fine material."

"What a sweet couple," Elsa said to Mark when they were alone again, getting ready to retire. "But I still wish I could have saved Carol from this awful experience."

"I'm sure it was good for both of them, Elsa. They'll learn that the church is made up of many kinds of people. Many of them don't even know what the church is supposed to be. I'm sure that one day Bill will be able to handle any situation."

"I just hope they won't have a Mr. Rollins in the future."

"I'm sure that is the nicest thing we can wish for them. I'm so angry with Rollins I could throw him out of the church and his money after him. I'll have to watch myself. I think I almost hate that man."

And Elsa couldn't blame him. Mr. Rollins had worked

against Mark in many ways. The banker could buy himself into anything, and he had to have his own way. The people who worked against him were almost always destroyed—and now his target was Mark and his work. Elsa wondered, as new days came and went, if her faith in the Church could ever be completely restored.

Mark and Elsa decided to try to forget the whole evening. But one day the subject arose when Carol dropped in for a morning visit.

"I can't get that Board meeting out of my mind, Elsa. Those men were perfectly horrible to Mark. And when I think of the long hours he has spent working on those apartments and all the counseling. . . . How awful to be belittled by your own congregation. I just can't live with the thought that these things happen."

"That, perhaps, is the hardest part of being a minister's wife, that you suffer with your husband. All his hurts are yours, too."

"I know, Elsa; I can feel it already and no one has ever been nasty to Bill."

"They will be, though, in time to come. At times you die a thousand deaths, but that's all part of it."

"How have you stood it all these years? And you're still willing to go on? Even if you have had fine churches, I know you must have been hurt many times."

"Yes, but, Carol, in the ministry there are many wonderful things that happen, too. At times it is almost a glamorous position. Most people are really quite dear and wonderful."

"You like being a minister's wife, don't you, Elsa?"

"I love it! I'm so much older than you, Carol, but take it from me, it is well worth the little troubles. And your husband needs you. Remember, dear, whenever your husband is down, you must be up. Don't ever join him down there at the bottom. Find a way to lift him up again. Often a minister experiences a crisis and a good wife can pilot him through without scars."

"You're so wise, Elsa! I have so much to learn, but I feel fortunate having someone like you to learn from."

"Thanks, Carol. Being a minister's wife is a great calling. In a way, it's very much like a nurse's relationship to a doctor. You stand beside him and you must know what he needs before he asks, and be ready to give it to him."

"Really, I've learned so much. Perhaps if that Board meeting had never taken place, you wouldn't have told me all these things. I know that at times I am selfish. I don't want to be left sitting alone while Bill goes off to the hospital to visit someone who's sick or dying. A minister's wife always has to come second; his work comes first. But I'll learn little by little; I'm beginning to understand a bit more about it now. I must make the grade. You see, Elsa, I am going to have to be more than a wife; I am going to be a mother, too."

Elsa put her arms around Carol. "I'm so happy for you and Bill. When is the baby due?"

"At the beginning of the year, when the snow falls and the wind blows in from the ocean. Bill and I are so excited and it's wonderful just to dream about it."

For a while they discussed babies and suddenly the gloom which had filled their hearts was gone. Carol wanted to know so many things and it was fun for Elsa to remember how things had been when she and Mark first became parents.

What a gift from God! There was nothing that compared to the thrill of knowing you were carrying a new life and looking forward to the day you would first cradle your child in your arms.

Long after Carol had gone, Elsa was still sitting on the sofa, smiling to herself. If any two people in the world deserved happiness, Carol and Bill did, and she hoped that every day of waiting would be filled with joy. What a good mother Carol would be. Elsa just couldn't wait for Mark to arrive home so she could tell him the news.

≈ 16

THIS COULD have been just another Sunday morning in the parsonage; the same stillness prevailed. The Cartlings, now a full family unit of five, had had a light breakfast together. Susan was off duty this Sunday and Gary was to join the family in time for church. Everything seemed the way it should be, but to Mark nothing was right. His soul was troubled and his body tired. He had tried to conceal his feelings from Elsa; she had been upset enough by the stormy Board meeting and he didn't want her to know how much that still bothered him. Mark had had many sleepless nights, twisting and turning in his bed. The wound was deep and painful. Nothing had ever hit him with quite as much force as this last blow—to think that church members could be so cruel and thoughtless! And lately he had wondered what he could do to earn a living if he left the ministry. He did not enjoy such thoughts, for he loved his calling, even now when it had turned

171

sour and bitter. He had even been asking himself if he was really a big enough man to fill this job.

This morning Mark decided to leave for church early. He would make sure his sermon was safely placed under the pulpit and then spend the remaining time meditating. His sermon had been written when he was angry and disillusioned, and in it he had stated clearly what he felt the congregation needed to hear. This sermon would not be popular, he thought, but those who would feel its impact were the guilty ones and they had it coming.

"I'm leaving early, Elsa," Mark called out. "I have things to do at the church. See you later."

Elsa went to the door with him. "Have a good Sunday, Mark! And take heart—all this will blow over before long. You said so yourself."

He guessed he hadn't fooled Elsa. She could see through him, no matter how hard he tried to cover up his feelings.

"I know that, dear," Mark gave her a light kiss. "I think I'll walk up the hill today. It's such a lovely morning."

It was a perfect June day—neither too warm nor too cool. The roses rambling along the stone wall were just opening into full bloom, and the birds were everywhere, singing as they gathered food for their young. Mark took long strides up the steep hill. Never had the church looked more inviting to him; the tall spire pointed graciously upward and the stained-glass windows reflecting deep rainbow colors. What a picture the church

172

made in the sunlight! Soon the bells would ring, calling the people to worship, and the chimes would fill the whole town with music.

Mark sat down on the marble steps for a minute to rest. As he studied the bits of blue ocean seen through the heavy foliage, a strange loneliness filled his heart.

Why had the awful meeting taken place? he wondered. Why did people take pleasure in hurting others? And why did some members of the church seem to thrive on destroying their preacher? That was what they were doing; they were destroying all that was sacred within him. For the first time in his life he dreaded the eleven o'clock service. How could he preach today? But he would because he had to. Had he not been reminded just recently of his more than adequate salary?

The hurt and bitterness festered in Mark. He tried to pray, but found no comfort. Even Heaven seemed closed to him today. He simply could not pray, not even to ask God for strength to preach His word to the people. Mark seemed lost in his own dark wilderness. His nerves were on edge, and his stomach was upset. Perhaps he was getting an ulcer.

There was still an hour before the service began. The chimes played and the tower bell marked the time. But even the beauty of the music did not soothe Mark's soul nor lift his spirit. He walked slowly to the dressing room off the foyer just outside of the sanctuary. Mechanically he slipped on his black robe and hung the hood around his neck. Then he slumped down in a chair by the window which overlooked the front walk. He gazed out at the people who were arriving early. The janitor, of course, was already there, and soon the choir director arrived, walking briskly, full of life and vigor. He looked like a stranger to Mark.

Funny, he thought, I don't even know that man. After three years in this church I've never had a heart-to-heart talk with him. We've only had short conversations about hymns and sermon topics.

The ushers arrived early too, one by one, from the parking lot. He did not know them well either. They were fine-looking men! Mark wondered if they hated him, too? Next came the Sunday-school teachers, carrying their textbooks and Bibles, ready to work with the children. He knew their names and where they lived, but nothing about their personal lives or if they were happy or sad, or if they struggled with problems too great for them. He did not know what went on inside them. He had been too busy with routine church duties and the apartments to find out such things. As the choir members began to drift in, Mark discovered that most of them were also strangers to him.

Then he watched the families who came early so they could sit together. Mark stared as if he were seeing these people for the first time. There were the Budds and their children. What a lovely family! Seven of them—and the young parents seemed so content and happy. He had been in their home only once but had been received warmly. That was at least two years ago. Mrs. Budd's mother, who was somewhere on the West Coast, had been ill and her daughter had been quite concerned about her. It occurred to Mark now that he had never followed up on it. Had the lady recovered or not? Had there been an item about her in the church bulletin sometime ago or was that Mrs. Lawson's mother?

Suddenly Mark sat up straight in the chair as new thoughts hit him. They were all strangers to him. He knew very few of his people personally and nothing of their spiritual lives. What kind of a shepherd was he anyway? What kind of a leader for God's flock? Had he given so much to the apartment people that he had neglected his own. No, that couldn't be true. But it was! Mark faced facts. He tried to face himself and his God. What he had done for the people in the apartments he would not have undone for any price, but could he have been so wrapped up in that work that he had never bothered to learn the thoughts of those he was hired to minister unto? Why else would they all seem like strangers? Even Mr. Rollins, whom Mark knew only as a pushy, self-centered, shrewd business-man, must have a side that Mark had not yet seen.

Mark was deeply shaken. It just couldn't be so! But if this were true, then he had wronged the church in the same way he had wronged David. He had judged his church members blindly, drawing his own conclu-sions about them without really knowing anything about them. It was not intentional. Mark had always thought he had fulfilled his obligations as a minister, but he obviously had not used the right methods. He should have had the same love and patience for his own

175

church members that he had had for the poor. He should have helped them see the need in the world, especially the world on Linden Street. Perhaps if he had taken them down there one by one, they, too, would have felt compassion. Instead of splitting the church, he should have drawn its people closer together by helping them to live their faith in a lost world.

Instead he had foisted on his congregation those unwanted people. He had never put himself in his members' place. In fact, if he were to be honest, he had taken a certain pleasure in seeing them uncomfortable. No wonder resentment was so evident. The Reiseners did not speak to the Andrews anymore and hostility was prevalent because he had forced them to take sides. This should never have happened in the house of the Lord. Suddenly Mark could see things so clearly. He had taken the wrong road. He should have loved his own people as much as he had loved the poor. Then he would have understood them. Because he had taken the time to look into the hearts of the unlovely, he had learned to understand and know them, and they, in turn, learned to know him. Now they loved him, which was the reason they flocked to his church.

Why hadn't he told them about his church, the way the people thought, how hard it was for the elite to accept other people's way of dressing and acting. Elsa could have helped the women find hats for Sunday if they didn't have them. There were plenty of rummage sales around town. And he could have helped the men find jackets for Sunday mornings. But no, when he

176

saw them sitting there hatless, in jeans and slacks, he had gloated. They're good enough for these stuffy rich, he had said to himself.

Now Mark saw himself, a self he had not taken time to discover before. It was as if a giant spotlight were shining on his own soul, and he was not pleased with what he saw. He had really failed in his calling. All he could do now was to step down. If he could not be a shepherd to all these people, then how could he serve as a minister?

For a moment he bowed his head, trying to pray, but no words came, only thoughts tumbling over each other. But a calmness had come over him, and in his mind he saw the Church of God in all its glory, stripped of selfish desire and filled with love. This was the Church he had told Mr. Johnson about, the Church founded on Christ with its responsibilities in the hands of believers, the committed. This was the real Church, not a building, but people all over the world working in separate patterns, but committed to the same cause—making all people members of the great kingdom of God.

People no longer were coming up the walk and the bell had stopped pealing. Mark heard the organ playing. It was time to go into the sanctuary, but he had no sermon to preach! After this last hour, the sermon under the pulpit was obsolete. Mark had been reborn! He could no longer lash out at his people. He could only love them. "May God help me to know what to do," he prayed.

177

His thoughts were interrupted by a soft knock on the door. His secretary stuck her head in.

"Forgive me for intruding, Mr. Cartling, but you are late. The organist is playing the hymn a second time, and the choir is waiting for you to join them."

Mark forced a smile. "I'm coming, Olive."

Mark filed in behind the choir and the procession up the long aisle began. The church was filled to capacity; every seat was taken. The choir took their places on either side of the pulpit, but Mark did not enter his pulpit. He stopped on the top step of the platform and turned to face the congregation. The organ stopped playing and Mark motioned to the people to be seated. A hush fell over the sanctuary and every eye was turned to Mark. Then he spoke. His words sounded like a recording to his ears, as though he spoke against his own will, but still his voice came strong and clear.

"Friends, I have a special request to make of you today. This service will be different from any we have held in this sanctuary. I am asking the choir not to sing this morning and the organist not to play. The ushers need not wait on the people and I am not going to preach. I am just going to stand here and talk to you for a few moments, sharing with you some startling realizations that have just been revealed to me. For the first time I have seen myself, as if a bright light has revealed my soul. I did not like what I saw—a person much too small to be a servant of the Lord. I feel I am not worthy to be a minister. You see, I also saw the Church—the real Church as it was given to the world by

178

Christ some two thousand years ago. It was a mysterious Church, but a glorious one, and its commitments then are equally relevant today. The shepherd of that flock was a committed man, a man who listened to the voice of God. The Church was not a building; it was made up of souls who had discovered the treasure of eternity, whose commission was to lead people out of the darkness into the light, to set men free through God's love. In comparison, I found myself unworthy and now I am not sure if I am the man God needs in this place. Where God is there should be unity, peace, togetherness, and love."

Mark paused for a moment. There was deathly silence. Mark met Elsa's eyes which were wide with bewildered concern.

"In this new light," he went on, "all I can see is that I have failed as a pastor. I worked hard, I admit, to serve God, but I know I have a lot more to learn about establishing a harmonious relationship between church and pastor——"

Before Mark could finish his thought, a man in the congregation stood. Mark knew him well. He was Peter Mason, a resident of the apartments.

"Excuse me, Pastor Cartling, for butting in like this, but if you are planning to resign, don't do it. We need you in our community. That is why I'm speaking up. So please wait a while longer until we are strong enough to stand on our own feet. I don't know if this congregation knows how much you have done for us down in the north end. For example, I was on my way to becoming

179

a bum, but you helped me to stop drinking and helped me get a job, thus saving my marriage. Now I have found a church home that I love. We owe much to this church. Your Fund for the Poor helped my family many times when I was on a drinking spree and we had no money. It often paid our rent and bought our food. And there are many others for whom the same thing was done. But the money didn't bring us beauty or love or self-respect or spiritual help. Since we got that, we haven't needed anyone to pay our rent. The people down there on Linden Street are happy now, and this is just the beginning. This is why I'm speaking, perhaps out of turn. Church life is new to me, but nothing must happen to the pastor who has been our liberator."

He sat down heavily, embarrassed at his own words. But his eyes searched Mark's face.

Mark opened his mouth to speak, but before he could do so, another man left his seat and hurried to the pulpit. Mark could not believe his eyes. It was James Rollins. Mr. Rollins coughed and cleared his throat noisily, then began to speak.

"If there is to be no sermon today, I will take this opportunity to say a few words both to the congregation and to Mr. Cartling, if he will kindly sit down for a few moments."

Mark would have liked to object. What in the world could Mr. Rollins have to say at a time like this?

But Mr. Rollins continued, "I can't understand what has happened to the orderly procedure of our service. But the congregation, I am sure, is not aware of the

180

strain our pastor has been under this last year. Unfortunately, much of what has taken place has been unpleasant and degrading for our church. We want to rectify that. We want to be a loving, serving church. I have had sleepless nights lately. My wife can bear me out on that. I, too, have seen a vision of myself, and I haven't liked what I saw either. I'm glad Mr. Mason spoke up. . . . Thank you, Mr. Mason, for opening my eyes this morning. . . . I would like to be one of those who are committed. I am no longer young, but I hope there is still time.

"It is strange how quickly a person can change his way of thinking. For a long time I have waged an undeclared war against Pastor Cartling. I did not like the way he took things into his own hands and pushed them through. I never stopped to think whether this apartment project was right or wrong. The whole idea aggravated me. You see, those apartments were my baby. I had started to rent them cheaply to the poor. I really felt that I was doing something as a Christian, something rather noble. Then when it was pointed out that the buildings were falling apart for lack of repairs, I thought that the people just didn't care about fixing things up, and if they wanted to live like that, it was up to them. After all, we were giving them a roof over their heads and heat in the winter. I am not a hard man.

"Mr. Mason spoke of our Fund for the Poor. If you are confused, you have every right to be. There is no such fund in our church treasury. The misconception is my fault. I wanted to do something for somebody, so it was I who paid the rent and bought food. The money came from my own account. At heart I have a soft spot for the poor because I was once poor myself, and I know how it feels. This was my secret gift to mankind; not even my wife knew about it.

"Oh, I told the pastor that if people did not pay their rent we threw them out. I guess I just wanted to sound gruff. No one has ever been evicted. But I loved myself for my charity. Not until now did I realize how selfish I have been. I guess that's why I didn't want those apartments torn down. They had been my pet project. But Pastor Cartling came and took that away from me. He gave the people what I never had the vision to give—love and beauty. I've been a pretty small character, I'm afraid, and we've all been poor neighbors to the people on Linden Street. We haven't been very friendly to them when they came here to worship with us, but all that is going to change, I'm sure.

"And don't worry, Mr. Mason. Our pastor will not resign. We shall all stand behind him and take up that commitment to help our fellow men and to serve God, not our church building. I know that everyone in this church loves the Cartlings. I'm afraid I'm the one who caused the discord among us . . ."

A tear rolled down Mr. Rollins' cheek and he brushed it off with the back of his hand.

"I want to admit to you here this morning that when the pastor stood in front of us a little while ago and said that he had been wrong, knowing of his love for us, and knowing the love he had poured out on the poor and needy, something within me melted. I felt that if Pastor Cartling could take blame on himself, I could, too. I could admit that I had been wrong, and suddenly I wanted to do that more than anything else in life. I wanted to make things right, which is why I decided to take over the service and open my heart to God and my fellow man. Now I feel happy. I know this was the right thing to do.

"This is the longest speech I have ever made in this church, but I hope I have made it clear that I feel like a changed man."

Mr. Rollins blew his nose loudly and, red with embarrassment, he turned to Mark. "Now, Pastor, perhaps you have another word for us—a good word, I hope. But in any case, please close this unusual service in a proper way."

Mark stepped to the pulpit—his pulpit. He felt as if his feet had wings and his heart beat with a happy rhythm. There was a broad smile on his face.

"What more is there to say?" he asked gently. "I think Mr. Rollins has preached the best sermon I have ever heard."

The organist began to play an old familiar hymn: "Onward Christian soldiers, marching as to war . . ."

The choir recessed and Mark followed them down the long aisle. As he passed Elsa and the family in the second row, he gave them a broad smile. Then, in a flash, David stepped out of the pew and joined his father. David's face was serious, but his eyes glistened.

"Dad," he whispered, "you were cool! Really great!

I want to walk down the aisle with you to see how it feels. Something funny happened to me this morning. Seeing you stand there stripping yourself of all glory and confessing that you had been wrong got me in the pit of my stomach. You were so honest. You really gave it to them straight. And the guy from the apartments—just the way he spoke made me proud of you —and then Mr. Rollins! Unbelievable! This has been the greatest day I can remember. Everything seems changed. Even the church seems different. It all made me feel that I want to be like you and reach people. For the first time, I feel something like a nudge toward the ministry . . . I'm not sure yet, Dad, but maybe one day you'll have a son walk in your shoes. *It could happen*, Dad, and I wanted you to know. . . ."

The organ played on, and the congregation seemed to be singing with a new fervor: "Like a mighty army, moves the Church of God . . ."

Mark took his son's hand. No, he would not cry. A man did not cry if he knew how to control his feelings. This was the happiest moment in his life, and he was sure it was a great moment for David, too. God must be pleased in his Heaven.

In the foyer the recessional stopped. The congregation was seated. There was a moment of silence and then with great sincerity, Mark Cartling lifted his hand for the benediction.